George Washington Doane

Songs by the Way

The Poetical Writings of George Washington Doane. Third Edition

George Washington Doane

Songs by the Way
The Poetical Writings of George Washington Doane. Third Edition

ISBN/EAN: 9783744768429

Printed in Europe, USA, Canada, Australia, Japan

Cover: Foto ©Andreas Hilbeck / pixelio.de

More available books at **www.hansebooks.com**

SONGS BY THE WAY.

THE

𝕻oetical 𝕸ritings

OF THE RIGHT REV.

GEORGE WASHINGTON DOANE, DD., LL.D.,

ARRANGED AND EDITED

BY HIS SON,

WILLIAM CROSWELL DOANE.

" Cantantes licet usque, (minus via lacdet) eamus."

" —— Sometimes a listless hour beguile,
Framing loose numbers."

" Where perfect sweetness dwells, is Cosmos gone,
But his sweet lays, to cheer the church, live on."

THIRD EDITION.

ALBANY:
JOEL MUNSELL.
1875.

A

Memorial of the Reunion.

The Graduates of St. Mary's Hall, present at the first Reunion, May, 1875, unanimously resolved :

That a Committee be appointed to wait upon the Bishop of Albany, and request a copy of his Father's Poems, for publication.

The Committee subsequently reported, that the Bishop had acceded to the request, as his memorial offering to the Reunion.

INTRODUCTION.

In an old wood, stands a great oak tree. It braves the winds, and courts the fury of the storm, and challenges the forked points of the lightning ; and keeps off, from the young trees and the new grass and the dear flowers, what would kill *them*, at the risk of its own life. This is its work. And, yet, it has time to shade the little children, and give them acorns for their play ; and time to make a winter home for squirrels, and a hive for the wild bees ; and time, to throw its leaves out, for coolness and for beauty ; and time, to change them, in the autumn glory, for our eyes to look on ; and time, to give its dry and withered leaves to God's great winter wind, to play its solemn music. And the leaves crown all. It is mighty in its roots, gnarled in its trunk, great in its branches. It can be a ship to carry the world's treasures, or a nation's armies ; it can be the arched roof of a cathedral. And yet, its Spring leaves are as tender as a sapling's ; its Summer emeralds, as green as the grass blades ; its Autumn colours, as deep, as though its only care were beauty. And the leaves are the crown of all. So God glorifies strength with beauty ; as, in the old fable, Venus was the wife of Vulcan ; and the highest human glory, of the greatest life, is God's adorning of a brave, great soul, with the loveliness, of grace and beauty. Such greatness, did He give my Father. And with the earnest seal, which death sets, on reverent and abiding love, this crown of the oak's own leaves — the beauty of a strong, enduring soul — hangs round the arms of the Cross, that marks his first and final rest.

My Father's poems were not the labour of his life. His own name for them, " Songs by the Way," is the best and truest name. Poems are creations. And in the truest sense, the creations of his life are poems, permanent and beautiful, in all their usefulness and strength. His poems either bloomed, out of the deep valleys of suffering, which duty made in his life ; or were the graceful vine, that grew, unsolicited, over the rough rocks, of his steep pathway into glory. His heart was full of them ; and when the rod smote the rock ; when he was touched by kindness, or by suffering, by a child's gift of a violet, or some heroic deed of a man ; they just flowed out, in all the force and fervour of nature and necessity. And, like all his life, they were all tributary streams, of that great ocean of worship, that gathers round the Church's Altar, and dashes its eternal waves against the very Throne of God. The hard workman, beguiled the weariest task, setting its labour, to the music of his soul.

Many of these verses were published, in A. D. 1824, in a volume now out of print ; bearing the title of this book. Many others, from time to time, have appeared in newspapers,— and there are many, beside these, whose echoes linger round his beautiful home, and in our loving hearts ; that will not go beyond those sacred shrines.

RIVERSIDE, *May* 15, *A.D.* 1859.

SONGS BY THE WAY.

MORNING.

" My voice shalt thou hear in the morning."

To Thee, O Lord, with dawning light,
   My thankful voice I'll raise,
Thy mighty power to celebrate,
   Thy holy Name to praise;

For Thou, in helpless hour of night,
   Hast compass'd all my bed,
And now, refresh'd with peaceful sleep,
   Thou liftest up my head.

Grant me, my God, Thy quick'ning grace,
   Through this, and every day,
That, guided and supported thus,
   My feet may never stray.

Increase my faith, increase my hope,
   Increase my zeal and love;
And fix my heart's affections, all,
   On Christ, and things above.

1

And when, life's labours o'er, I sink
 To slumber, in the grave,
In death's dark vale, be Thou my trust,
 To succour and to save ;

That so, through Him who bled and died,
 And rose again, for me ;
The grave and gate of death, may prove,
 A passage, home, to Thee.

NOON.

"At noon will I pray."

FATHER of lights, from Thee, descends,
 Each good, and perfect gift ;
Then hear us, while our thankful hearts,
 In songs of praise, we lift ;

We praise Thee, Maker, that Thou, first,
 Didst form us, from the clay ;
And gav'st us souls, to love Thy name,
 To worship, and obey.

We praise Thee, that the souls Thou gav'st,
 Thou, still, in life dost hold :
Preserver, noon would fade to night,
 Ere half Thy love, were told !

We praise Thee, Saviour, that Thou didst
  Our souls, from death release,
And, with Thine own atoning blood,
  Procure us, endless peace.

Maker, Preserver, Saviour, God !
  What varied thanks, we owe
To Thee, howe'er addressed ; from Whom,
  Such varied blessings flow :

To Thee, who on a darken'd world,
  Celestial light, hast pour'd ;
And told of heav'n, and taught the way,
  In Thy most holy Word.

Wide, as the blaze of noon is spread,
  Spread Thou, that Word abroad :
We ask it, Saviour, in Thy name ;
  Maker, Preserver, God.

———

EVENING.

Psalm cxli. 2.

[1] SOFTLY now the light of day
  Fades upon my sight away ;
  Free from care, from labour free,
  Lord, I would commune with Thee :

[1] Since inserted among the hymns in the Prayer Book.

Thou, whose all-pervading eye,
   Naught escapes, without, within,
Pardon each infirmity,
   Open fault, and secret sin.

Soon, for me, the light of day
   Shall for ever, pass away ;
Then, from sin and sorrow, free,
   Take me, Lord, to dwell with Thee :

Thou, who, sinless, yet hast known
   All of man's infirmity ;
Then, from Thine eternal throne,
   Jesus, look with pitying eye.

MIDNIGHT.

"*God my Maker, who giveth songs in the night.*"

At midnight hour, O Lord, I wake,
   To think upon Thy name ;
To call to mind Thy gracious acts,
   And all Thy praise, proclaim ;
And though no friendly ray should shine,
Nor single eye should wake, but mine,
My spirit knows no startling fear,
Convinced that Thou, my God, art near.

Thou, in my time of deep distress,
   Didst aid me, from on high ;
Didst wipe the starting tear, away,
   And still the bursting sigh :
Life cannot throw so deep a gloom,
There is no darkness in the tomb,
Can e'er disturb my breast with fear,
For Thou, my God, wilt still be near.

THE VOICE OF RAMA.

"Rachel weeping for her children, and would not be comforted."

HEARD ye from Rama's ruined walls,
   That voice of bitter weeping ?
Is it the moan, of fetter'd slave ;
   His watch, of sorrow, keeping ?
Heard ye, from Rama's wasted plains,
   That cry of lamentation ?
Is it the wail of Israel's sons,
   For Salem's devastation ?

Ah, no, a sorer ill, than chains,
   That bitter wail, is waking ;
And deeper woe, than Salem's fall,
   That tortured heart is breaking :
'Tis Rachel, of her sons bereft ;
   Who lifts that voice of weeping ;
And childless are the eyes, that there,
   Their watch, of grief, are keeping.

Oh ! who shall tell, what fearful pangs,
    That mother's heart, are rending ;
As o'er her infant's little grave,
    Her wasted form is bending ;
From many an eye, that weeps to-day,
    Delight may beam, to-morrow ;
But she, her precious babe is not !
    And what remains, but sorrow ?

Bereaved One ! I may not chide
    Thy tears, and bitter sobbing ;
Weep on ! 't will cool that burning brow,
    And still that bosom's throbbing ;
But, be not thine, such grief as theirs,
    To whom, no hope is given :
Snatched from the world, its sins and snares,
    Thy infant rests, in Heaven.

———

"I am the Way, and the Truth, and the Life." [1]

THOU art the Way; to Thee alone,
    From Sin, and Death, we flee;
And he, who would the Father seek,
    Must seek Him, Lord, by Thee.

[1] Since inserted among the hymns in the Prayer Book. A few nights before Bishop White died, as my Father was watching at his bedside, he asked him to read this hymn.

Thou art the Truth; Thy word alone,
  True wisdom, can impart;
Thou only canst inform the mind,
  And purify the heart.

Thou art the Life; the rending tomb,
  Proclaims Thy conquering arm,
And those who put their trust in Thee,
  Nor death, nor hell, shall harm.

Thou art the Way, the Truth, the Life;
  Grant us, that Way to know,
That Truth, to keep; that Life, to win;
  Whose joys, eternal flow.

THE WATERS OF MARAH.

"And Moses cried unto the Lord; and the Lord showed him a tree, which, when he had cast into the waters, the waters were made sweet."

By Marah's stream of bitterness,
  When Moses stood and cried,
Jehovah heard his fervent prayer,
  And instant help, supplied:
The Prophet sought the precious tree,
  With prompt, obedient feet;
'Twas cast into the fount, and made
  The bitter waters sweet.

Whene'er affliction, o'er thee sheds
　　Its influence malign,
Then, sufferer, be the Prophet's prayer,
　　And prompt obedience, thine :
'Tis but a Marah's fount, ordained,
　　Thy faith in God, to prove ;
And prayer and resignation shall
　　Its bitterness, remove.

———

"Our Father, who art in Heaven."

" Our Father—" such Thy gracious name,
Though throned above the starry frame,
Thy holy name, be still adored,
Eternal God, and Sov'reign Lord :
Spread far and wide, Thy righteous sway ;
Till utmost earth, Thy laws, obey ;
And, as in Heaven, before Thy throne,
So here, Thy will, by all, be done :
This day, Great Source of every good,
Feed us, with our convenient food :
As we, to all, their faults forgive,
So bid us, by Thy pardon, live :
Let not our feeble footsteps stray,
Seduced by sin, from Thy right way :
But, saved from evil work, and word,
Make us Thine own, Almighty Lord :

For Thine the sceptre is, and throne,
    That shall be crush'd, or shaken, never ;
The glory Thine, O God, alone,
    And power that shall endure, for ever.

———

"Lord, I believe : help Thou mine unbelief."

" Lord, I believe," the father cried ;
    " Help Thou mine unbelief :
O ! if Thou canst, have mercy now,
    And give my child relief !"

The father's fervent prayer was heard,
    Fulfill'd, the father's joy ;
The Saviour pitied, spake, and healed
    His poor demoniac boy.

Sinner, this Lord is still the same,
    Still waiting, to forgive ;
Seek, then, His cleansing, saving blood,
    Believe, obey, and live.

Sufferer, it is thy Father smites,
    Thy Father's chastening love :
The hand that gives, will heal the wound,
    In fairer realms above.

2

Christian, 'tis there thy Saviour reigns,
 Enthroned above the skies,
And thither, freed from death's dark thrall,
 Thy ransom'd soul shall rise.

Believer, press undaunted on,
 Nor heed earth's dull delay,
While angels wait, to welcome thee,
 To realms of ceaseless day.

Sinner, no more, nor sufferer then,
 Life's painful journey o'er,
Thine is the Christian heritage
 Of joy, for ever more;

And crowns of quenchless glory thine,
 Thy constancy's reward;
Believer, thine, in Heaven to dwell
 Forever with the Lord.

———

THE LOVE OF CHRIST.

" Who shall separate us from the love of Christ ? "

SHALL tribulation's deep distress,
Or fear, or want, or nakedness,
Or cruel foe, or conquering sword,
Divide us, from thy love, O Lord ?

No, vain alike, were death, and life,
  And powers of hell, and Satan's strife,
And things that are, and things to be,
  To separate us, Lord, from Thee !

So shall we, Saviour, through Thy love,
  In all things, more than conquerors prove;
Nor grave shall hold, nor hell shall harm,
  The ransom'd of Thy holy arm.

THE FAITHFUL SAYING.

"This is a faithful saying, and worthy of all acceptation, that Christ Jesus,
came into the world, to save sinners."

YES, it is a faithful saying,
  Christ, the Saviour, died for me :
Haste my soul, without delaying,
  To His great atonement, flee.

Shall the Lord of earth and heaven,
  Sojourning with sinful men,
Die, that they may be forgiven,
  Yet his death, be all in vain ?

No, by every drop, that's streaming
  Down, from that accursed tree,
By Thy death, my soul redeeming,
  Saviour, I will come to Thee !

Worldly riches, honours, pleasures,
　　Shall no more, my soul detain;
Dearer, Thou, than all the treasures,
　　Earth can give, or life can gain.

THE SINNER CALLED.

RETURN, and come to God,
　　Cast all your sins away,
Seek ye the Saviour's cleansing blood,
　　Repent, believe, obey.

Say not, ye cannot come,
　　For Jesus bled, and died,
That none, who ask in humble faith,
　　Should ever be denied.

Say not, ye will not come
　　'Tis God, vouchsafes to call,
And fearful, shall their end be found,
　　On whom, His wrath shall fall.

Come, then,　whoever will,
　　Come, while 'tis called to-day,
Flee to the Saviour's cleansing blood,
　　Repent, believe, obey.

" In the hour of death, and in the day of judgment."

My God, when nature's frame shall sink,
And totter on destruction's brink,
Be Thou my portion, and my cup,
And bear my fainting spirit, up.

For Thou didst form me first, from clay;
Hast led me, through life's devious way;
Then take, O God, my parting breath,
Support me in the hour of death.

And when before the throne I stand,
And wait Thy judgment's dread command,
Do Thou, my strong supporter, be,
And save the soul, that trusts in Thee.

Thou, Saviour, for my sins hast died,
Thy grace alone, my strength supplied;
Then cast me not, O Lord, away,
But save me, in the judgment day.

THE PLAGUE OF DARKNESS.

" But all the children of Israel had light in their dwellings."

When darkness erst, by God's command,
Enveloped haughty Egypt's land,
Throughout that long and fearful night,
In Israel's dwellings, all was light.

So, to the righteous, light shall rise,
Though clouds and tempests wrap the skies,
And faith, triumphant, mock the gloom,
That gathers round the silent tomb.

Then grant us, God, while here we rove,
Thy will to know, Thy ways to love,
To prove the riches of Thy grace,
And share the brightness of Thy face;

Till, guided, so in all our way,
And cheered by Thy celestial ray,
We reach, at last, that heavenly height,
Where all is peace, and joy, and light.

———

"Lord, to whom shall we go ? Thou hast the words of eternal life."

LORD, should we leave Thy hallowed feet,
    To whom should we repair ?
Where else, such holy comforts meet,
    As spring, eternal, there ?

Earth has no fount of true delight,
    No pure, perennial stream ;
And sorrow's storm, and death's long night,
    Soon wrap life's brightest beam.

Unmingled joys, 'tis Thine to give,
  And undecaying peace ;
For Thou canst teach us, so to live,
  That life shall never cease.

Thou, only, canst, the cheering words
  Of endless life, supply,
Anointed, of the Lord of Lords,
  The Son of God, most High.

———

THE WATER OF LIFE.

"Whosoever will, let him take the water of life freely."

Ho ! all that thirst, draw nigh,
  And drink of that pure fount,
Which issues forth eternally,
  From Zion's holy mount.

Haste to that blessed fold,
  Which Jesus first ordained,
And which, His hand and holy arm,
  Have ever since maintained.

There, shall the sacred Fount,
  Wash all your sins away,
And fit you, so your faith be firm,
  For realms of endless day.

There, is that Word dispensed,
　By which alone, we live,
Which only can our hopes confirm,
　And joys eternal, give.

There is that Feast prepared,
　For those in Christ who live ;
Rich banquet ! where the contrite heart
　True comfort shall receive.

Come, then, the Spirit cries,
　And she, the heavenly Bride,
Come, all that are athirst, nor fear
　That one shall be denied.

Come, whosoever will,
　Nor price, nor money bring ;
Come to that fount, whose streams of life
　Through endless ages, spring.

————

"The fashion of this world passeth away."

In careless childhood's sunny hours,
　When all we love, is nigh,
No thorn, amid life's opening flowers,
　No cloud, in all its sky ;

We fear no ill, nor dream of care,
   But deem, each following day,
Shall light us, on, to fairer scenes,
   And beam, with brighter ray.

And childhood's vernal season past ;
   And shunned youth's thousand snares,
When manhood's autumn comes at last,
   With sorrows, fears, and cares,
Still, autumn-like, its skies are bright,
   And still, the world seems young,
And still, we love its mellow light,
   Its bowers, with fruitage hung.

But autumn's golden skies must fade,
   And autumn's fruits decay,
And soon, 'mid snows and storms, must come
   Old age's wintry day.
A wintry day at best, as short,
   As gloomy, and as cold,
Till the worn body yields at last,
   And life lets go its hold.

And when its earthly hold is gone,
   The world's brief fashion past,
Are there no hopes, that shall survive,
   No pleasures, that shall last ?
Yes, Christian, it is thine to know,
   Life's but a weary way,
A short, though painful, pilgrimage,
   To realms of endless day ;

3

Where Faith, her crown of life, shall wear,
   And Hope, be lost in joy,
And meek-eyed love, be paid with bliss,
   That time can ne'er destroy :
For thither, has the Lamb gone up,
   Who suffered, and was slain,
That, risen with Him, His followers might
   With Him, for ever, reign.

———

TO A VERY DEAR FRIEND.[1]

"——— Friendship, I owe thee much."

DARK to the soul, and desolate,
   Life's sunniest hours would be,
And cheerless, fortune's best estate,
   Fair Friendship ! but for thee.
And oh ! when tempests wrap the skies,
   How comfortless, their gloom,
Did not thy radiant visions rise,
   Our darkness to illume !

Friend of my heart ! in hours of joy,
   I've listened to thy voice ;
And felt, in each inspiring tone,
   New motive, to rejoice ;

[1] The venerable Rector of Trinity Church, New York, the Rev. Dr. Berrian.

And oft, with anxious cares oppressed,
   And griefs, thou didst not know,
Thy kindness has relieved my breast,
   And lightened every woe.

Oh ! I have loved, with thee to rove,
   In Spring's reviving hour,
Ere verdure yet, had clad the grove,
   Or fragrance filled the flower ;
And joyed, when Summer found us laid,
   Beneath some aged oak,
Where, save the streamlet's bubbling tale,
   No sound, the stillness broke.

With thee, when Autumn's mellowing hand
   Has tinged the woods with gold,
How dear, to mark each varied tint
   Successively unfold !
And e'en in Winter's sullen hour,
   To roam, delighted, on,
And feel, that not in Summer bower,
   Is nature wooed, alone.

Those happy hours, those happy hours,
   Have flitted on the wind ;
But many a dear remembrance lives,
   Deep in my heart, entwined ;
And oft, the chords with which they're bound.
   Shall fancy wake again ;
And memory love to linger long,
   Delighted, on that strain.

LIFE'S LITTLE LINES.

"Noting, ere they fade away,
    The little lines of yesterday."

LIFE's "little lines;" how short, how faint,
    How fast they fade away;
Its highest hopes, its brightest joys,
    Are compassed, in a day.

Youth's bright, and mild, and morning light,
    Its sunshine, and its showers,
Its hopes and fears, its loves and tears,
    Its heedless, happy hours;
And manhood's high and brightened noon,
    Its honours, dangers, cares,
The parents' pains, the parents' joys,
    The parents' anxious prayers;
Fade in old age's evening gray,
    The twilight of the mind;
Then sink, in death's long, dreamless night,
    And leave no trace, behind.

Yet, though so changing, and so brief,
    Our life's eventful page,
It has its charms, for every grief,
    Its joys, for every age.

In youth's, in manhood's, golden hours,
    Loves, friendships, strew the way
With April's earliest, sweetest flowers,
    And all the bloom of May;

And when old age, with wintry hand,
   Has frosted o'er, the head,
Virtue's fair fruits, survive the blast,
   When all beside, are fled ;
And faith, with pure, unwavering eye,
   Can pierce the gathered gloom;
And smile upon the spoiler's rage,
   And live, beyond the tomb.

Be ours, then, virtue's deathless charm,
   And faith's untiring flight ;
Then shall we rise, from death's dark sleep,
   To worlds of cloudless light.

———

THERMOPYLÆ.

Σᾶς περί, παρθένε, μορφας,
Καί θανεῖν ζαλωτὸς ἐν Ἑλλάδι πότμος.

'Twas an hour of fearful issues,
   When the bold three hundred stood,
For their love of holy freedom,
   By that old Thessalian flood ;
When, lifting high each sword of flame,
They called on every sacred name,
And swore, beside those dashing waves,
They never, never, would be slaves !

And Oh ! that oath was nobly kept :
　From morn, to setting sun,
Did desperation urge the fight,
　Which valour had begun ;
Till, torrent-like, the stream of blood
Ran down, and mingled with the flood,
And all, from mountain-cliff, to wave,
Was Freedom's, Valour's, Glory's grave.

Oh, yes, that oath was nobly kept,
　Which nobly, had been sworn ;
And proudly, did each gallant heart
　The foeman's fetters spurn ;
And firmly, was the fight maintained,
　And amply, was the triumph gained ;
They fought, fair Liberty, for Thee ;
They fell ; to die is to be free.

———

" And I said, Oh ! that I had wings like a dove ; for then
　would I flee away and be at rest."

WHO that has mingled in the fray,
　Or borne the storms of life,
Has not desir'd to flee away
　From all its sin and strife ;
Has not desir'd to flee away,
　Like yonder startled dove,
And seek, in some far wilderness
　A nestling-place of love ;

Where the tumult, if heard, should excite no alarm,
And the storm and the tempest sweep by without harm ?

Who that has felt the rankling wound
Of disappointment's sting,
Or prov'd the worse than vanity
Of every earthly thing,
Has not desired, like yon sweet dove,
To wander far away,
And find some desert lodging-place,
And there forever stay,
Where the vain show of earth should no longer delude,
Where the fiend disappointment should never intrude ?

Who, that has felt the crumbling touch
Of premature decay,
Or, sorer far, has mourned o'er friends
Torn from his heart away,
Has not desir'd like yonder dove
To seek some lonely nest,
And, far from earth's vain fellowship,
To dwell and be at rest,
Till the summons be heard that shall bid him depart,
And forever rejoice the beloved of his heart ?

And it shall be, that summons of joy shall be giv'n,
To the converse of saints, to the mansions of Heaven,
Where the cross of the suff'rer shall no more be borne,
But the crown of the conq'ror forever be worn.

' Tis the promise of Christ, to the poor shall be given,
And humble and contrite, the kingdom of Heaven,

And who would not toil through this pathway of pain,
And who would not suffer, such promise to gain !

Bear up then, my soul, 'mid the darkness and storm,
Nor shrink from the strife, tho' terrific its form,
There is One that shall guide thee and guard thee from harm,
Whose eye is unerring, unconquered His arm.

To the contrite and faithful, the promise is sure,
And salvation is pledg'd to the souls that endure,
And the crown and the sceptre shall be their reward,
Who have manfully stood on the side of the Lord.

Thou that seek'st this glorious prize,
    Ask no more for wings of dove,
Angel-pinioned thou shalt rise,
    To the realms of peace and love.

Realms, where Christ has gone before,
    Blissful mansions to prepare ;
Realms, where they who serve Him here,
    Shall His power and glory share.

There, no battle-fray is heard ;
There, no tempest need be feared ;
Disappointment cannot sting ;
Banish'd thence each hurtful thing ;
Sickness comes not there, nor pain ;
Death hath there no dark domain ;
Gathered there, no foot shall rove
Of the happy friends we love ;
Gathered there, no soul shall roam :
'Tis our own, our Father's Home.

FRAGMENT.

'Twas night—and winds were raving round,
With stern December's surly sound ;
The well-swept hearth was burning bright,
And shed on all its cheering light ;
The doors were closed, the curtains drawn,
The floor-cloth smooth as verdant lawn,
And all was joy, and sportive mirth,
Around the dear domestic hearth.

Domestic love ! what holier shrine,
Save One, is reared on earth, than thine ?
Where, as when clustered round thy feet,
Does heart meet heart, in concord sweet ?
Star of our souls where'er we roam,
We turn to thee, delightful home !

'Twas night—the feather-footed hours
Had fled, as if they " stepped on flowers ;"
Had noiseless fled, yet left behind
In happy hearts, mementos kind
Of hours, in social converse spent,
When every look is eloquent
Of moments passed, with those we love,
Prized by the heart, long years, above :
Moments, which shall for ever be,
Embalmed in fondest memory.

4

The jest, the laugh had circled round,
Mingled with music's silver sound;
That wild and witching melody
   Which moves, at once, and melts the soul,
And bids, from out the unconscious eye,
   The involuntary tear-drop roll.
Such notes as oft, at midnight hour,
   The sad enthusiast, ravish'd, hears;
Far echo of some angel's song,
   Sweet harmony of circling spheres.
Those notes, those notes, they linger yet,
Oh ! who that heard them, could forget !
Speech shall be lost, and thought, as soon
As that sweet voice, and " Bonny Doon."

ROSEMARY.

" There's rosemary,— that's for remembrance !"

It is not the brightest and sweetest flow'r
   That the heart of affection may longest cherish;
For when the winds rise, and the tempests low'r,
   The fairest is ever the first to perish;
Oh no, the wither'd and wild-wood leaf
   Is as dear to the heart, for it will not vary;
And dear, e'en the straw from the oaten sheaf,
   And the simplest sprig of the sad rosemary.

The rosemary, friendship's strongest charm,
   " Seeming and savour the winter long,"
Through the year's chill night it receives no harm,
   Nor fades, though the tempest beat loud and strong ;
And so will the heart, with affection warm,
   In joy and in sorrow be ever the same,
And the blink of the sun, and the dash of the storm,
   What are they all to its changeless flame !

They say that the rosemary leaf can shed
   On the mem'ry that's fading, a magical pow'r ;
And, sweetly embalming the past and the dead,
   With the dew of remembrance, their life restore ;
Oh ! thus when the light of affection's smile
   Has beacon'd me over the world's rough wave,
May the dew of its tears, when my voyage is done,
   Freshen the green of my turf-covered grave.

REMEMBERED JOYS.

" Sweet mem'ry ! wafted by thy gentle gale,
Oft up the stream of life I turn my sail,
To view the fairy haunts of long-lost hours,
Blessed with far greener shades, far fresher flow'rs."

Remember'd joys, remember'd joys,
   With what a soft and " dying fall "
Ye breathe upon the bosom, where
   " Hope comes no more, that comes to all ;"

Recalling pleasure's wildest strains,
    Divested now of all their madness,
And grief's subduing melodies,
    With scarce a single tone of sadness.

Remember'd joys—to those who keep
Their vigils sad, while others sleep;
To eyes unseen, that ceaseless weep,
    And watch the lingering night away,
How dear the calm delights you give !
Departed lov'd ones seem to live,
Departed scenes again revive,
    Returns again youth's golden day;
And slowly as the visions move
Of youthful friendship, early love,
    Before the enthusiast's charmed eyes,
His swelling heart forgets its pain,
He breathes his childhood's air again,
He treads once more his native plain,
And gleams of bright-haired hope again before him rise.

Dim twilight of remember'd joys,
    I would not give one gleam of thine,
For all the gaudy world can yield,
    When most its noontide splendours shine.
Clouds may obscure life's brightest days,
    And, rainbow-like, its hopes depart,
      But oh ! the joys of other years,
      Enshrin'd by love, embalm'd with tears,
Till mem'ry leaves her latest hold,
    Shall live unalter'd in my heart.

THE FADED FLOWER.

The flower you gave, oh! lady fair,
   Pale as it seems, and scentless now,
Is dearer than the loveliest rose
   That blooms on Summer's gaudy brow.
The loveliest rose but blooms awhile,
   And wafts its precious perfumes round ;
The gale sweeps by, it charms no more ;
   Its scattered leaflets strew the ground.

Not so the little flower you gave ;
   Its bloom may fade, its fragrance flit,
But oh ! the charm affection lends,
   And mem'ry loves, will linger yet :
Will linger yet — long years have pass'd,
   The storm has fall'n, the gale swept by :
Still, is it fragrant to my heart,
   Still, blooming to my memory.

There is a bloom no time can fade,
   There is a fragrance will not part ;
It lives unchanging in the breast
   It breathes unfailing in the heart.
That breast, unnumbered ills may wring,
   That heart may bleed, perchance be broken ;
In all alike, it still shall charm,
   That faded flower, that cherished token.

THE HEART'S TRIBUTE.

TO AN ABSENT FRIEND.[1]

"Wi' melting heart, an' brimfu' eye,
"I'll mind you still, tho far awa."

WHEN friends are met, and beaming mirth
    Is throned in every eye,
Why wanders oft, the absent thought,
    And starts, the secret sigh ?
'Tis the silent tribute, of heart to heart,
    Which affection loves to pay,
And 'tis wafted off, on that secret sigh,
    To the friends that are far away.

And why, amid its wreathéd smiles,
    Turns pale that cheek with fear ?
And why, beneath that joyous brow,
    Lurks oft, the gushing tear ?
'Tis to wet the graves of departed joys,
    That the heart, that big tear, sends ;
And the fear, that pales that anxious cheek,
    Is the fear, for absent friends.

There's ONE, his name's in all our hearts,
    For whom, where'er he be,
Our kindest thoughts, our fondest prayers,
    Are wafted o'er the sea :

[1] The Rt. Rev. Bishop Hobart.

May the spirit of health, be on every breeze,
   And of joy, in every ray,
And may God, in mercy, protect the friend
   Whom we love, while far away !

HOME.

"The music of Carrol was like the memory of joys that are past, pleasant, but
mournful to the soul."— *Ossian.*

HOME of my careless infancy,
   How dear each well-remembered scene,
Where every rock, and every tree,
   Is eloquent, of what has been.

How dear, yet ah ! how painful too;
   That joy, how near to grief, allied,
When thoughts of loved ones, now no more,
   Come rushing on me, like a tide.

Departed joys, of days gone by,
   As slowly on, your visions roll,
My heart is softened, and subdued ;
   Ye soothe, and tranquillize my soul.

Like music, wafted on the gale,
   When midnight stillness wraps the land,
So sweet the far-off strains ye breathe,
   So sad, when waked by memory's hand.

"FORGET ME NOT."

FORGET thee ! how could I ? each morn would remind me,
  Of days, which thy presence has hallowed and blest,
And each night, in its visions and dreams, would restore
      thee,
  All pureness and beauty, mine angel of rest.

Forget thee ! why should I ? since with thee, is blended,
  Each scene of delight, that my fancy e'er drew,
And the hopes, that on thee, and thy love, have attended,
  Were those of my life, I most wished to find true.

No, trust me, that fervent and fond recollection,
  Those hopes, even fonder, can never depart,
Till the holiest fount of my earthly affection
  Shall ebb, with the warm tide of life, from my heart.

SONS OF THE GREEKS.

Δεύτε παῖδες τῶν Ἑλλήνων.

"Sons of the Greeks, arise !"
  And gird your armour on ;
Your bleeding country's rights assert,
  Avenge your fathers' wrong.

Sons of the helméd brave
  Who held Thermopylæ,
Dare, as they dared, the turbaned slave,
  And Greece shall yet be free.

Shades of the brave, who bled
  Along Cithaeron's steep,
And still, round glory's hallowed bed,
  Your watch of ages keep;
Say — shall yon tower-crowned hill
  No more be Freedom's home ?
Her flag, no more, in triumph float,
  Amid yon ocean's foam ?

Yes ! soon again as pure,
  Ilissus' wave shall flow,
And soon, on famed Hymettus' hills,
  As fragrant flowers shall blow;
For freedom's sun shall rise
  On Attica once more,
And wind and wave, shall lash and lave,
  The *free* Ægean shore.

Shades of the mighty dead,
  Whose ashes still repose,
Where Œta rears his star-girt head,
  Where cold Eurotas flows,
Inspire each patriot's heart,
  To dare, as you have dared,
Till nerved be every manly arm,
  And every falchion bared.

5

Light, light the quenchless flame,
  In every warrior's eye ;
Rouse, rouse the glorious battle-cry,
  For Greece — for Victory !
Nor let the combat cease,
  While Moslem shall remain
To mar fair Freedom's festal rites,
  Her heritage, to stain.

Hark ! 'tis the trumpet's clang,
  The squadron's tramp, I hear ;
Clashes, the bright broadsword, again,
  And ring, the shield and spear :
See ! 'tis the pluméd helm,
  The banner streaming wide ;
The Athenian horsemen mount again,
  And Spartan, side by side.

'Tis up — the glorious strife,
  By field, and tower, and town ;
And palace, mosque, and minaret,
  And frowning fort, are down :
The Ottoman retreats,
  The Crescent veils its ray,
And holy hands, in Stamboul's streets
  The cross of Christ display.

" Sons of the Greeks arise !"
  Rise in your fathers' might,
With sword girt on, and spear in rest,
  Wage Freedom's holy fight ;

Swear — 'twas the father's oath,
And well befits the son —
Swear, free to live, or firm to die,
" By those in Marathon !"

———

THE MOURNED — THE LOVED — THE LOST.

WHY, on the vanished look, the by-past tone,
    Loves the fond heart, devotedly to dwell ?
Why, reckless of that *now* which is its own,
    Of hours that *were*, delights it still to tell ?

Why, for its pillaged nestling mourns the dove,
    With all her living loves, still all unblest ?
Why dotes the fond, bereaved mother more
    On her dead infant, than on all the rest ?

Why is it, that around the loved and lost,
    Her most enchanting radiance, fancy throws,
While all the past is robed in richer green,
    And fresher fragrance breathes from every rose ?

Mysterious Sympathy ! thy sacred source,
    Thy deep, embosomed springs, we cannot tell,
Nor scan thy subtle, undetected laws,
    Though each effect, we feel and know so well.

'Tis thine, the withered floweret, most to prize,
  To mourn the music flown, the odour shed ;
And, in the hallowed tomb of buried love,
  To twine life's best affections, round the dead.

ON A VERY OLD WEDDING RING.

The Device — Two hearts united.
The motto — "Dear love of mine, my heart is thine."

I LIKE that ring, that ancient ring,
  Of massive form, and virgin gold,
As firm, as free from base alloy,
  As were the sterling hearts of old.

I like it, for it wafts me back,
  Far, far along the stream of time,
To other men, and other days,
  To men and days, of deeds sublime.

But most I like it, as it tells
  The tale of well-requited love ;
How youthful fondness persevered,
  And youthful faith disdained to rove.

How warmly *he* his suit preferred,
  Though *she*, unpitying, long denied ;
Till, softened and subdued at last,
  He won his " fair and blooming bride."

How, till the appointed day arrived,
 They blamed the lazy-footed hours;
How, then, the white robed maiden train,
 Strewed their glad way, with freshest flowers;
And how, before the holy man,
 They stood, in all their youthful pride,
And spoke those words, and vowed those vows,
 Which bind the husband to his bride;
All this it tells; the plighted troth,
 The gift of every earthly thing,
The hand in hand, the heart in heart;
 For this, I like that ancient ring.

I like its old and quaint device;
 "Two blended hearts,"—though time may wear
  them;
No mortal change, no mortal chance,
 "Till death," shall e'er in sunder tear them.
Year after year; 'neath sun and storm,
 Their hopes in heaven, their trust in God,
In changeless, heartfelt, holy love,
 These two the world's rough pathways trod.
Age might impair their youthful fires,
 Their strength might fail, 'mid life's bleak weather,
Still hand in hand, they travelled on;
 Kind souls! they slumber now together.

I like its simple poesy too:
 "Mine own dear love, this heart is thine!"
Thine, when the dark storm howls along,
 As when the cloudless sunbeams shine.

" This heart is thine, mine own dear love !"
    Thine, and thine only, and for ever ;
Thine, till the springs of life shall fail,
    Thine, till the cords of life shall sever.

Remnant of days departed long ;
    Emblem of plighted troth unbroken ;
Pledge of devoted faithfulness ;
    Of heartfelt, holy love, the token ;
What varied feelings, round it cling !
    For these, I like that ancient ring.

———

THAT SILENT MOON.

That silent moon, that silent moon,
    Careering now, through cloudless sky ;
Oh ! who shall tell, what varied scenes
    Have passed beneath her placid eye ;
Since first, to light this wayward earth,
She walked, in tranquil beauty, forth !

How oft, has guilt's unhallowed hand,
    And superstition's senseless rite,
And loud, licentious revelry,
    Profaned her pure and holy light :
Small sympathy is hers, I ween,
With sights like these, that Virgin Queen !

But dear to her, in summer eve,
　By rippling wave, or tufted grove,
When hand, in hand, is purely clasped,
　And heart meets heart, in holy love ;
To smile in quiet loneliness
And hear each whispered vow, and bless.

Dispersed along the world's wide way,
　When friends are far, and fond ones rove,
How powerful she, to wake the thought,
　And start the tear, for those we love,
Who watch with us, at night's pale noon,
And gaze upon that silent moon.

How powerful too, to hearts that mourn,
　The magic of that moonlight sky,
To bring again the vanish'd scenes —
　The happy eves of days gone by :
Again to bring, 'mid bursting tears,
The loved, the lost of other years.

And oft she looks, that silent moon,
　On lonely eyes, that wake to weep,
In dungeon dark, or sacred cell,
　Or couch, whence, pain has banished sleep :
Oh ! softly, beams her gentle eye
On those who mourn, and those who die !

But beam, on whomsoe'er she will,
　And fall, where'er her splendours may,
There's pureness, in her chastened light,
　There's comfort, in her tranquil ray :

What power is hers, to soothe the heart —
What power, the trembling tear to start !

The dewy morn, let others love,——
   Or bask them, in the noon-tide ray ;
There's not an hour, but has its charm,
   From dawning light, to dying day : —
But oh ! be mine a fairer boon,
That silent moon, that silent moon !

Translations and Imitations.

MORNING HYMN.

" Rex sempiterne cœlitum."

MAKER of all in Heaven and earth,
   Lord of the hosts on high,
Thou Son, Who, with the Father, art,
   From all eternity,
'Twas Thou, Who, when the world was new,
   Creating man, of earth,
Didst give him, in Thine image made,
   A soul of heavenly birth.

And when by spite and fraud of hell,
   That image was decayed,
Veiled in the flesh, 'twas Thou restor'dst,
   The soul, Thyself hadst made.

Great Shepherd, Who Thy flock dost wash
   In baptism's sacred wave;
Be this the pool, to cleanse our souls;
   · Of all our sins, the grave;
That, buried there, with Thee, we may
   With Thee, our life resume,
Who, of a Virgin born, wast made
   The first fruits of the tomb.

6

Redeemer, Thou, who, to the cross
  Due to our sins, wast led,
And there, salvation's countless price,
  Thy precious blood didst shed ;
Do Thou, our souls, renewed to life,
  From sin and death, set free,
That thus, Thy endless joy, O Lord,
  Our heritage, may be.

Then to the Father, and the Son,
  Who rose, and reigns in Heaven,
And to the blessed Comforter,
  Shall ceaseless praise be given.

HYMN.

FOR THE SEASON OF LENT.

" Audi, benigne Conditor."

FATHER of Mercies, hear !
  Thy pardon, we implore,
While daily, through this sacred fast,
  Our prayers, our tears, we pour.

Searcher of hearts, to Thee,
  Our helplessness is known ;
Be then, to those, who seek Thy face,
  Thy free forgiveness, shown.

Our sins have numerous been,
 We own it, Lord, with shame;
Yet spare, and heal, the broken heart;
 Spare, for Thy glorious name.

Grant us, the body so,
 By fasting, to restrain,
That sinful thoughts, and vain desires,
 Our souls, no more may stain.

Thus, to Thy contrite ones,
 Thy mercy shall be shown;
We ask it, blessed One in Three,
 We ask it, Three in One..

MORNING HYMN.

" Ecce jam noctis tenuatur umbra."

THE shades of night are flitting fast,
 The golden east is streaked with day,
And now, O Lord of life, and light,
 With thankful hearts, to Thee we pray.

Sinners we are, yet hear us, Lord
 In pity hear, and send us peace;
Thy saving health, to all afford,
 And bid each sin and sorrow cease.

Grant it, eternal Trinity,
  The Father, Son, and Spirit blessed,
Whose glory is, and still shall be,
  Through all the world, with joy, confessed.

———

MORNING HYMN.

" Jam lucis orto sidere."

WITH dawning light, O Lord, to Thee,
  On bended knee, we pray,
That Thou, from every hurtful thing,
  Would'st keep us, through this day.

Guard Thou, from guile, our froward tongue,
  Lest sinful strife arise ;
Guide Thou our feeble, erring sight,
  Lest vanity entice.

Cleanse, Lord, our hearts from every sin,
  Free them, from folly too,
And let continual temperance,
  Each carnal lust, subdue :

That so, when days shall dawn no more,
  Nor nights, their shadows fling,
Free from the world, and all its stains,
  Thy praises, we may sing.

For Thou, O God! and Thou alone,
 Art worthily adored.
Who, with the Son, and Spirit, art
 But one Almighty Lord.

To Him, therefore, be glory given,
 Whom, Virgin Mother bore,
With Father, and with Holy Ghost,
 Both now, and evermore.

MORNING HYMN.

"Consors Paterni luminis."

BRIGHTNESS of the Father's glory,
 Light of Light, unclouded day,
Lo! we rise, to sing Thy praises;
 Hear us, help us, while we pray.

Lighten Thou, our mental darkness,
 Bid each hellish tempter, flee,
Rouse our dulness, lest it deaden
 Our devotions, Lord, to Thee.

Saviour, deign to each believer,
 These, Thy favours, to extend;
Answered thus, our prayers and praises
 Shall, for evermore, ascend.

Hear us, Father, we intreat Thee,
　　Hear us, Saviour, we implore,
Hear and help us, Holy Spirit—
　　Thou, that reignest evermore.

———

MORNING HYMN.

"Tu Trinitatis unitas."

THREE in One, and One in Three,
　　Sovereign of the Universe,
Hear our morning minstrelsy,
　　Listen to our thankful verse.

From our couches, lo ! we rise,
　　Seeking 'mid the darkness still,
Help for our infirmities,
　　Medicine for every ill.

If in dreams, by Satan's fraud,
　　Thought or wish hath gone astray,
Let Thy glorious power, O Lord,
　　Wash the secret sin away.

Keep our bodies free from stain,
　　Keep our hearts from coldness free,
Let no taint of vice inflame,
　　Our spirits dedicate to Thee.

Thus, Redeemer, while we pray,
  Fill us with Thy heavenly light,
Then, throughout each circling day,
  Thoughts and deeds shall all be right :
Aid us Father, we intreat ;
  Aid us, Thou, eternal Son ;
Aid us, Spirit, Paraclete —
  One in Three, and Three in One :
Thou, in our behalf engage,
Thou, that reign'st from age to age !

      ———

HYMN FOR NOON.

" Rector potens, verax Deus."

God of truth, Almighty King,
Lord of each created thing,
Thou that light'st the dawning day,
And kindlest high the noontide ray ;

Quench in us each flame of strife,
Banish ev'ry ill of life,
To each body health impart,
Shed Thy peace on every heart.

Grant it now, O Holy One ;
Grant it, Thou, eternal Son ;
Grant it Spirit, we implore,
Thou that reignest evermore.

EVENING HYMN.

"Jam sol recedit igneus."

Now, as sinks the blazing sun,
Thou, eternal Three in One,
Fountain of unclouded day,
Fill us with Thy purer ray.

Thee we praise at morning's dawn,
Thee implore when eve comes on
Grant us, suppliant here, to raise
In Heaven, unmingled songs of praise.

Thus, the Father, and the Son,
And the Spirit, Three in One,
As of old, shall ever be
Praised and worshipped, One in Three.

EVENING HYMN.

"Te lucis ante terminum."

Creator of the world,
  As now the day departs,
We ask it for Thy mercy's sake,
  Guide Thou, and guard our hearts.

Let no foul forms of night,
  In dreams our souls beguile,
Nor suffer, Lord, our mortal foe
  Thy temples to defile.

O Holiest ! grant it now,
  And Thou, co-equal Son,
And Thou, O Spirit Paraclete,
  Eternal Three in One.

HYMN FOR WHITSUNDAY.

" Veni, Creator Spiritus."

Come, Holy Ghost, Creator, come,
And make these souls of ours Thy home ;
Come, fill our hearts with grace divine,
Thou mad'st them — own them still as Thine :
To Thee, our Comforter, we cry,
The gracious gift of God most High :
Thine is the unction from above,
The living fount, and fire of love ;
Sevenfold Thy sacred blessings are,
God's promises Thou dost declare,
Hand of the Father, stretched to give
That blessed Word by which we live.

7

Oh kindle, Thou, each sluggish sense,
Thy love in all our hearts dispense,
Strong in Thy strength, grant us to bear
Those ills to which our flesh is heir.
Drive far away each spiteful foe,
And give us peace while here below,
That, led by Thee, O Holy One,
Our feet each sinful snare may shun.

Grant us the Father now to know,
    And Son eternal to confess,
And Thee, who from them both dost flow,
    Through every circling year to bless;
That so, to Him who spoiled the grave
    And rose triumphant up to Heaven,
With Father, and with Holy Ghost,
    Eternal glory may be given.

————

EVENING HYMN.

"Verbum supernum prodiens."

Eternal Word, Who dost proceed
    From out the bosom of our God,
And cam'st, in hour of utmost need,
    To shield us from th' avenging rod,

O, lighten Thou our darkened hearts,
  Inflame us with celestial love,
And, as life's empty show departs,
  Fill us with comforts from above.

Then, when the uplifted judgment seat
  The sinner's sentence shall display,
And voices, as of angels sweet,
  Welcome the saints to realms of day;
For us no quenchless flame shall rage,
  No fiery storms our rest destroy;
Thy favour, Lord, our heritage,
  Thy presence our exceeding joy.

And now to Father and to Son,
  And Spirit, Paraclete, to Thee,
The One in Three, the Three in One,
  Be praise throughout eternity.

MORNING HYMN.

"Veni Creator Spiritus.

Creator, Spirit, come
  Visit these souls of Thine,
And fill the hearts, Thyself hast made,
  With influence divine.

Thou Comforter art called,
  The gift of God above;
The spiritual unction Thine,
  The fount and fire of love.

Send down Thy holy fire,
  Pour out Thy heavenly love
And bear us in our frailty up,
  With succours from above.

Drive far away each foe,
  And give us peace at home
Be Thou our guardian and our guide,
  And ills shall never come.

———

EVENING HYMN.

" Creator alme siderum."

Creator of the starry frame,
  Light of the souls who trust in Thee,
Jesus, Redeemer of mankind,
  To Thee we call on bended knee.

Thou, when the tempter's arts prevailed,
  Didst hasten down on wings of love,
To shield and save a ruined world,
  With health and peace from heaven above.

And Thou, unspotted paschal Lamb,
  The Blessed Virgin's holy Son,
To wash our souls from stain of sin,
  On shameful cross didst bleed and groan.

Exalted now, Thy glorious power
  Extends through all immensity,
And saints in heaven, and fiends in hell,
  Bow at Thy name with trembling knee.

To Thee, then, judge of all, we look ;
  Grant us Thy heavenly help, we pray ;
Guide us in life, and guard in death,
  And shield us in the judgment day.

For Thine the glory is, and power,
  Eternal Sire, eternal Son,
Eternal Spirit ; Thine the praise,
  The One in Three, the Three in One.

FOR THE FESTIVAL OF THE HOLY INNOCENTS.

"Salvete flores Martyrum."

The jealous tyrant hears
  That He, the Prince, has come
Who wide o'er Israel's tribe shall rule
  From David's royal home.

Infuriate then, he cries,
  " He's come, who claims my throne ;
" Go, soldiers, grasp the glittering steel,
  Instant, with blood each cradle fill,
    Slay every new-born son."

Vain was murderous Herod's word ;
Vain was soldier's dripping sword ;
Safe, while all were slaughtered round,
God's anointed was not found.

Hail, infant sufferers — martyred flowerets hail !
  Cut off by ruthless knife,
  Even at the gate of life,
Ye fell, as new-blown roses fall, when scattered by the gale,
Earliest of all were ye, that suffered for the Word ;
Sweet firstlings of that slaughtered flock, so precious to the
    Lord :
And round His heavenly altar now, His high, uplifted throne,
Ye guileless sport the crown and palm, your martyrdom hath
    won.

    Therefore to Him be glory given,
      Whom Virgin Mother bore,
    With Father, and with Holy Ghost
    One God forevermore.

FROM THE LATIN OF SENECA.

" Stet quicunque volet."

Let him stand, whoever will,
On promotion's slippery sill.

Me let quiet satisfy,
Sweeter for obscurity ;
Finding every real pleasure
In a bland and blessed measure.

By the world of men unknown,
Let my life flow silent on,
So, when all its days are past,
Each more tranquil than the last,
Let me fill an old man's grave,
No man's master, no man's slave.

    Heaviest on him doth lie
    The burden of mortality,
    Who, known to all the world beside,
    Stranger to himself hath died.

Horace 3 : 13 of Odes.

" O fons Blandusiæ, Splendidior vitro."

Blandusian fount, Blandusian fount,
   Worthy of flowers and choicest wine,
To-morrow shall thy glassy wave
   Be honoured with this kid of mine.

E'en now his budding front he rears,
E'en now for love and war, prepares
In vain — for with to-morrow's sun
His brief career shall all be run,
Poor wanton ! and his burning blood,
Empurple then thine icy flood.

Fair fountain ! thee the dog star's rage,
   At sultry noon can n'er molest,
The wandering flocks, the share-worn herds,
   Delighted here in coolness rest,
And while the bard enraptured sings,
The spreaking oak, that o'er thee springs,
The arched rock, the rugged steep,
From which thy babbling waters leap,
What nobler stream wide earth can lave,
Blandusian wave, Blandusian wave !

SONNET :

FROM THE ITALIAN OF PETRARCH.

" La vita fugge, e non s'arresta un 'ora."

Life flits away without a moment's rest,
   And death with rapid strides comes hastening on ;
The past, the present, rend my aching breast,
   The future will, when they shall both be gone :
Memory and hope, alike, by turns perplex,
   And, truly, did I not sometimes forbear,
And cease, with anxious fears, my soul to vex,
   Such thoughts, long since, had pierced it through with
      care.

I look before me — and my aching heart
   Sometimes a single cheering ray descries,
'Tis vain — for instant on some other part,
   Fierce winds to whelm my wave-worn bark arise ;
And when the port is gained, and Fortune won,
   Wearied and wrecked, each ray that gilds her throne is
     gone.

————

FROM THE ITALIAN QF METASTASIO.

"La speme de malvagi."

The hope of the wicked —
A moment shall blast it,
When the breath of Jehovah
In wrath hath o'er passed it.

Like smoke, which the winds in their fury are lashing,
Or foam on the ocean when tempests are dashing,
It was — it is not — all its glories are o'er,
And the places that knew it, shall know it no more.

But the hope of the just
Is established forever,
For God is their trust,
And that trust shall fail — never.

The heavens at the voice of His thunder may shake,
And earth at the flash of His lightnings may quake,

8

But their hope and their trust
   Shall be ever the same,
Unfailing, unchanging,
   Jehovah, His name.

TO THE PENINSULA OF SIRMIO.

FROM THE LATIN OF CATULLUS.

"Peninsularum, Sirmio, insularumque."

FAIREST of all Peninsulas,
   Eÿelet[1] of islands, Sirmio !
Of all the wide wave bathes, the best,
   Where'er its varied waters flow :
So glad, so joyful my return,
   So fondly I revisit thee,
I scarce can feel, that Thynia left,
That, from Bithynia's valleys reft,
Thee, once again, I safely see,

Oh ! feels the heart a happier hour,
   Than when, its every sorrow fled,
Thrown now aside, its painful load,
Accomplished now, its weary road,

[1] Ocelle, little-eye, — a term of endearment. So Cicero; villulæ meæ, ocelli Italiæ.

Reached now, the land that gave it birth,
Its native home, its holy hearth,
  It rests upon its own, its long, long, wished for bed ?
    Oh ! this, for toilsome road and rough,
    And labour hard, is meed enough,

    Hail, then, lovely Sirmio !
      Smile once more, upon your lord ;
    Lydian waves, that round me flow,
      Your murmuring welcome, now afford :
    Every smile you have, my home !
      Sport it now ; the wanderer's come.

———

TO GROSPHUS.

FROM THE LATIN OF HORACE.

"Otium divos rogat in patenti."

WHEN tempests turn the day, to night,
And clouds obscure pale Luna's light,
The sailor, 'mid Ægean seas,
No star to guide him, prays for *ease*.
For *ease*, the warring Thracian prays,
And Media's quiver-bearing race—
Ease, that no gems, nor gold can buy,
Nor robes, my friend, of Tyrian dye.
For, not the hoarded wealth of kings,
Nor state, that titled office brings,

Can drive those carking cares aloof,
　　Those vultures of the mind,
　　That riot unconfined,
And flit unscared, untamed, around the vaulted roof.

How happy he, though small his hoard,
Whose plate ancestral decks his board,
Whose tranquil sleep, no fears molest,
Nor lawless love, deprives of rest!

Rash, short-lived beings, that we are,
Why cast we still our schemes afar?
Why haste, from clime to clime, to range?
Himself, did exile, ever change?
No; *care* will climb the brazen poop;
Care still pursues the mounted troop;
Care; that is swifter than young hind,
Or clouds, that scud before the wind.

Blest then to-day, seek not, to borrow,
One anxious moment, from the morrow;
But soothe each grief, with gentle mirth;
Unmingled bliss dwells not, on earth.

Each has his lot.　Achilles died,
'Mid all his fame, in manhood's pride,
While old Tithonus pined away,
Year after year, in dull decay;
And I, though poor, perhaps may see
Long years, denied to wealth and thee:

Thee, purple-robed, whose heifers low,
   Whose well-trained steeds delighted neigh,
   Whose countless flocks securely stray,
Where'er Sicilian waters flow;
While, for my share, (so fate ordains,)
This little farm alone remains.

Enough! Since with it, I inherit
Some sparklings of the Grecian spirit;
   A mind not always slighted by the muse —
A soul that spurns the mob, and virtue's path pursues.

SONNET.

FROM THE ITALIAN OF TASSO.

"Donna, crudel fortuna a me ben vieta."

FATE binds me here: beloved one, farewell;
   Yet binds not all; the fond and faithful heart
   Bursts all restraint, and wheresoe'er thou art,
Its best affections, still, delight to dwell.
To deem thee pensive, now; now, light of heart,
   Now on the wave, and now, along the shore,
   Amid earth's stillness deep, or ocean's fitful roar;
Is faithful Fancy's never-tiring part.

And when, the circle of rejoicing friends
   Greet thee, with many a smile, and sportive kiss ;
   Half pleased, half envious of that lavished bliss,
One jealous pang, swift messenger, she sends :
   Home to the heart, the pained affections turn,
   And mingled grief and love, the throbbing bosom, burn.

THE PLEASURES OF A COUNTRY LIFE.

FROM THE LATIN OF HORACE.

" Beatus ille qui procul negotiis."

How blest is he, who, free from care,
As once, 'tis said, even mortals were,
Unknown to brokers, bonds, or bills,
His own paternal acres, tills.
No midnight storm along the deep,
Nor brazen trump, to break his sleep ;
Far from the Forum's pompous prate,
And thresholds of the lordly great ;
The wanton vine, 'tis his, to wed,
To poplar trim, with lofty head ;
And, pruning off each worthless shoot,
Engraft the slip, from choicer root.
Sometimes, where yonder vale descends,
His lowing herds, at ease, he tends ;
Shears, now, his sheep, with tottering feet ;
Now, stores the hive's delicious sweet ;

And now, when autumn smiling round,
Erects his head, with fruitage, crowned,
Plucks, with delight, the melting pear,
Or purple grape, of flavour rare;
What thanks, and offerings then recall
His care, who gives, and guards them all!

Sometimes, where streams are gliding by,
Stretched on the grass, he loves to lie,
Beneath some old and spreading oak,
Where rooks reside, and ravens croak,
While crystal fountains murmur round,
And lull his senses, with their sound.
But, when the raging winter god
Has sent his snows, and storms, abroad,
He scours the country, round and round,
To rouse the boar, with horse and hound;
With subtle art, his traps and nets,
To catch the tender thrush, he sets;
Lays for the crane, some stouter snare,
Or takes, delicious treat! the hare.
'Mid sports like these, unknown to ill,
What love, can cross! what cares, can kill!

But happiest then, if, while he roam,
His wife and children dear, at home —
(A modest matron she, and fair,
Despite alike of sun and air) —
The swelling udder, duly drain,
And close the sheltering fold, again:

Pile high, with seasoned wood, the fire,
To warm and dry, their wearied sire ;
Then, filled one small, but generous cup,
The unbought banquet, quick serve up.

Such fare be mine ! I ask no more ;
No shell-fish, from the Lucrine shore ;
No turbot rare, nor, driven from far,
By eastern winds, the costly char.
Oh ! not the fowl, from Afric shore,
Nor grouse, from Asiatic moor,
Were half such luxury, to me,
As olives, plucked from mine own tree ;
A dish of dock, that grows in fallows ;
A dainty mess, of wholesome mallows ;
A joint, on high and holy days,
Of roasted lamb, my board to grace ;
And, now and then, a rescued kid,
Which ravening wolf, had stolen and hid.

'Mid feasts like these, to sit, and see
My flocks wind homeward o'er the lea ;
The sober ox, returning first,
With languid neck, and plough reversed ;
And men and maids, the farm-house swarm,
Around the hearth-stone, gathered warm.
" What life so blest !" cried wealthy B——,
" I'm done with stocks.   A farm for me !"
Cash, loaned at *five*, called in ; he went,
And—put it out, at *six* per cent !

HARMODIUS AND ARISTOGEITON.

FROM THE GREEK OF CALLISTRATUS.

Εν μύρτου κλαδὶ τὸ ξίφος φορήσω.

I'LL wreathe my sword, with myrtle ; as the brave Harmo-
dius did,
And as Aristogeiton, his avenging weapon hid,
When they slew the haughty tyrant, and regained our liberty,
And breaking down oppression, made the men of Athens
free.

Thou art not, loved Harmodius, thou art not, surely dead,
But to some secluded sanctuary, far away art fled,
With the swift-footed Achilles, unmolested there to rest,
And to rove, with Diomedes, through the islands of the
blest.

I'll wreathe my sword with myrtle ; as Aristogeiton did,
And as the brave Harmodius, his avenging weapon hid,
When on Minerva's festival, they aimed the glorious blow,
And, calling on fair freedom, laid the proud Hipparchus
low.

Thy fame, beloved Harmodius, through ages, still shall
brighten,
Nor ever shall thy glory fade, beloved Aristogeiton,
Because your country's champions, ye nobly dared to be,
And striking down the tyrant, made the men of Athens free.

9

TO FUSCUS ARISTIUS.

FROM THE LATIN OF HORACE.

"Integer vitæ, scelerisque purus."

THE man, my friend, whose hands are pure
Needs not the shaft of tawny Moor;
Nor, armed with innocence of heart,
Asks he, the bow or venomed dart.
His way may lie o'er sandy plains,
'Mid hills, where desolation reigns,
By fabled stream, or haunted grot,
Secure in all, he needs them not.

For me, as, musing, late I strayed
In yonder Sabine forest's shade;
And, casting to the winds, all care,
Thought, but of Lalagé my fair;
A wolf; such horrid portent roves
Not all Apulia's warlike groves;
Not such, fierce Mauritania's coast,
Dry-nurse of monsters, e'er could boast;
Lone as I was, and quite unarmed,
Took flight and left me all unharmed.

Place me henceforth, 'mid polar fields,
Where earth no vegetation yields;

'Neath cloud-wrapt skies, where not a breeze
Wafts health and fragrance through the trees;
Or, where the tropic's ceaseless blaze
Blasts all that basks beneath its rays;
I'll fear no ill; but think the while,
Of Lalagé's bewitching smile;
Dear to my heart, she still shall be,
My sweetly-speaking Lalagé.

SONNET.

FROM THE ITALIAN OF PETRARCH.

" I'vo piangendo i miei passati tempi."

OH ! I must ever weep the years I've spent,
　Years, whose whole business and delight was love,
When, not an effort stirred those pinions, lent
　To spurn the ignoble crowd, and soar above.
Thou, who my errors and my crimes hast known,
　Great King of Heaven, eternal and unseen,
Aid my frail spirit, wandering here alone,
　And cleanse it, graciously, from every sin.
Grant that my life, 'mid storm and battle, spent,
　In peaceful haven, may at last repose;
If this be vain, whate'er its brief extent,
　Vouchsafe at least no ignominious close:
And oh ! in death, do Thou, my portion, be,
For, Lord, Thou knowest, my hopes are all in Thee.

TO THE SPRING.

AN IDYL.

FROM THE GREEK OF MELEAGER.

χειματος ἠνεμόεντος ἀπ' αἰθέρος οἰχομένοιο.

SEE, waked by stormy Winter's parting wing,
Smiling, 'mid flowers, comes on the purple Spring;
While verdant herbage crowns the dusky earth,
And new-leaved plants are joying, in their birth;
While fertilizing dews refresh the ground;
And early roses bloom and blush, around.
Glad, o'er the hills, the shepherd's pipe we hear,
Where snow-white flocks, in frolic mirth, career:
Cheerly, his ocean-path, the seaman hails,
While favouring zephyrs fill his swelling sails:
The Bacchants now, with clustering ivy, crowned,
Invoke the genial god, with jocund sound:
Their cells of purest wax, prepared with skill,
The careful bees, with dripping nectar, fill:
Now, wake the feathered tribes, their tuneful notes;
The queen-like swan, as down the stream she floats,
The halcyon, hunter of old Ocean's coves,
The swallow, twittering from the roof, he loves,
And Philomel, enchantress of the groves.
And say, while leaves, and buds, and flowers rejoice,
And teeming earth lifts up her glorious voice;

While shepherds warble their delighted lay,
And well-fleeced flocks their sportive gambols, play ;
While seaman shout, and Bacchants, joyous, throng,
And bees, their labour ply, and birds, their song:
Shall I, no strain, to earth's glad chorus, bring ?
Shame to the Son of Song, that hails not thee, O Spring !

INSCRIPTION,

FOR THE TOMB OF A LITTLE GIRL, EIGHT YEARS OLD.

"Οὐκ ἔϑανες, Πρώτη, μετέβης δ' ἐς ἀμείνονα χώραν."

No—I will not deem thee dead, my love, but parted far
 away,
Through fairer scenes than earth can yield, for evermore to
 stray ;
To dwell where ceaseless pleasures reign, in undecaying rest,
Amid the quiet shades of some far island of the blest.

And there, I ween, thy little feet, from every ill removed,
In frolic mirth now wander, as in infancy they loved ;
And still thy little heart exults amid Elysian bowers,
And still thy little fingers pluck the sweetest, fairest flowers.

Oh ! winter comes not there, to chill, with short and
 cheerless day ;
Nor summer suns are there, to scorch, with fierce and sultry
 ray ;

Nor hunger there, nor thirst, is known, to mar thine hours
    of ease ;
Nor, raging in his thousand shapes, the tyrant, fell Disease.

And shall I, though thou'rt torn from me, my precious one,
    repine ?
Alas ! how poor life's best estate appears, compared with
    thine —
With thine, who, far removed from all that dims its darkened
    ray,
Dwellest amid the splendours pure of heaven's unclouded ray.

WHY WISH FOR LIFE ?

FROM THE ITALIAN OF METASTASIO.

" Perché bramar la vita."

Why wish for life ? has this vain world,
    One source of pure delight,
Whose every fortune has its pang,
    And every age, its blight ?

Trembling, in childhood, at a look,
    In youth, with love's vain fears,
Man walks awhile, the sport of fate,
    Then sinks, oppressed with years.

'Tis now the strife to win, that racks
　His inmost soul with pain ;
And now, far worse, the fear to lose
　What cost so much to gain.

Thrones have their thorns ; eternal war
　Must gain them, and must guard ;
And envy, still, and scorn are found,
　Fair virtue's best reward.

Vain world ! whose dreams and shadows mock,
　Whose follies cheat the eye,
Till age, the base delusion, shows,
　Just time enough — to die.

LOVE AND DEATH.

FROM THE LATIN OF ALCIATUS.

" Errabat socio Mors juncta Cupidine."

Love and death, odd cronies they,
Met once, on a summer's day :
Death, his wonted weapons bearing,
Little love, his quiver wearing ;
　This to wound, and that to slay,
Hand in hand, they took their way.

Night came on.   The self-same shed
Furnished both with board and bed;
While, beneath a wisp of hay,
Heads and points, their arrows lay.
Ere the morning's faintest dawn,
Each had girt his armour on :
But with too much haste arranged,
Luckless chance ! their darts were changed.

Little space our heroes ran,
Ere their archery began.
Love, a whizzing shaft, let fly
At a youth, with beaming eye :
The aim was true ; one shriek he gave,
And sunk, into an early grave.
Death shot next ; he pierced the core
Of a dotard, past threescore :
The cankered carle, his crutch threw by,
A lover now, with amorous eye.

" Ho !" cried young Love, " here's some mistake ;
These darts of mine, sad havoc make."
" And mine," said Death, " instead of killing,
Serve but to set these bald-heads billing."
Reader, oft will *wanton age*
Bring to mind, our sportive page ;
Oh ! that *youth's untimely fall,*
Its sadder strain, should e'er recall !

TO DELIUS.

FROM THE LATIN OF HORACE.

Æquam memento rebus in arduis.

THOUGH adversity should harm thee,
    Still thy equal mind maintain ;
Though prosperity should charm thee,
    Be not insolently vain :
For whether clogged with sadness, life's brief moments pass
    us by,
Or winged with wine and gladness, still, my Delius, we must
    die.

    Where the pine and poplar blending,
        Fling their hospitable shade,
    And the limpid stream descending,
        Gently murmurs through the glade,
Bring the wine, and perfume rare, with the rose's short-
    lived flower,
While the fatal sisters spare, and life lends a summer hour.

    For soon the world resigning
        Thou shalt leave thy house and lands,
    And the well-piled treasures shining,
        To thy heir's delighted hands :
Nor shall fields, dear bought, avail thee, lashed by Tiber's
    yellow wave,
Nor thy noble birth preserve thee, from the dark and narrow
    grave.

10

Oh ! think not then 'twill matter thee,
    How low soe'er thy lot ;
Nor deem that death would flatter thee,
    Though royally begot !
Whether palace, rich and rare, should receive thy every breath,
Or it flit in open air ; it is all the same to Death.

To his rule we all are destined
    Whether soon or late our turn :
Nor may its lot be questioned—
    That inexorable urn ;
Nor the boat that wafts us over, to that undiscovered shore,
From whose eternal exile, we return again no more.[1]

1819—1825.

"Since, where thou art, I may not dwell,
'Twill soothe to be, where thou hast been."

FARE thee well, dearest, peace be thine,
    Though my lone day be dark, with sorrow,
May each of thine, more brightly shine,
    And happier still, thy every morrow.
Yes—round thy heart, may joy and peace,
    Contentment's garland, greenly wreathe,
Its buds of peace, each day, increase,
    And every floweret, sweeter breathe.

[1] These poems, in the order in which they are here (with a few others), appeared in the first edition of " Songs by the Way " published in New York, by E. Bliss and E. White, 128 Broadway, in A. D. 1824.

Farewell—thou goest to spread delight,
   Where'er thy peaceful presence beams;
And tho' the light, that blessed my sight
   With warmest ray, no longer gleams;
Yet, fare thee well; in joy and woe,
   The heart, that long has loved thee dearly,
No change can know, where'er it go,
   But still must dote on thee, sincerely.

And, when no more, that soft blue eye,
   Light of my way, life's beacon-star,
With cheering rays, around me plays,
   Nor throws its moonlight smile, afar;
Oh, then, each loved and lonely scene,
   I'll haunt, where thou wert wont to dwell;
And sweetly dream, and fondly deem;
   I hear thee say, " Farewell,—Farewell !"

Sept. 4, 1819.

" A glove, a shoe-tie, or a flower let fall,
   What tho' the least — Love consecrates them all."

AND canst thou ask me, why this rose
   Is held, so precious, by my heart ?
And knowest thou not, that Love bestows
     On slightest gifts, the faded flower,
     The severed lock, a mystic power,
   Can ne'er depart ?

And canst thou ask me, what the charm,
  That makes this withered rose, so dear ?
And why, preserved from hurt or harm,
    While other flowers have fallen, unwept,
    Like sainted relic, this is kept,
  Year after year ?

And canst thou ask me, what the worth,
  Which can attach to thing like this ?
And why, what seems like merest earth,
    What finds no grace, in eye of thine,
    Should be so doted on, by mine,
  In secret bliss ?

Then thou hast never felt the power,
  Of ceaseless, solitary love ;
Hast never known, how every hour,
    Spent with that one beloved alone,
    Will still be prized, when years have flown,
  All hours, above.

Aye prized ; though that were idle word,
  To speak the fond and fixed delight,
Which hangs on each soft accent heard,
    Each look dwelt on, as if the last,
    Each well remembered moment, passed,
  In her loved sight.

Then hast thou never known, what charm,
  Love to least relic, can impart ;
Nor how, like vine that's sheltered warm,

It spreads its tendrils more and more,
And twines still closer, than before,
Round the fond heart.

Years may roll on.   Stern fate may blight
The loveliest visions of the heart ;
Then, as such relic meets the sight,
Fond memory, on the past, will dwell,
And hope, of happier hours, will tell,
Hours, ne'er to part.

Oh ! not the flower in blooming pride,
At times like this, will most delight :
Gazed on, by many an eye beside,
Admired by some, and praised by all,
Its common charms, but cheaply fall,
On Love's sad sight.

Then, emblem of his own sad lot,
The heart that loves, and loves unblessed,
Will prize the flower by all forgot,
Wrest it from elemental strife,
And press it, like a thing of life,
To his own breast :

And keep it there ; that faded rose,
Shut from the cold, and common world ;
Till cherished long, at last it grows,
Part of his life, his fondest care,
Like magic word, which none may hear,
None, e'er hath heard.

But oh ! if once, in happier hours,
    When life was young, and earth seemed heaven,
When every step was stepped on flowers,
        And all, to his delighted eyes,
        Seemed fair, as primal Paradise,
    That flower was given,

By her, who shed on all this scene,
    Its light, and life, and loveliness ;
Whose eye, his star of hope, had been,
        Her smile, the mild and mellowed ray,
        That cheered his heart, and lit his way
    To happiness :

Think then, how round his heart of hearts,
    Relic of love, that flower would twine;
Nor, dearest, ask, tho' time departs,
        Though wavelike, year is rolled on year,
        Why cherished still, and still, more dear,
    This rose of thine.

1823.

———

"To say — I've thought of thee."

And is it so ? And hast thou thought,
    Beloved one, of me —
Deep, in my bosom's inmost cells,
    That thought shall treasured be:

And often, to that secret haunt,
  Shall memory repair,
To watch, with more than miser's joy,
  The wealth, that's buried there.

At midnight, shall that blessed thought,
  Compose my throbbing heart,
And bid the spectre-cares, that haunt
  That holy hour, depart ;
And when the morn, rejoicing, brings
  Its glad and golden ray,
That recollected thought shall lend,
  New lustre, to the day.

Yes, Mary ! deep within my breast,
  It shall forever lie :
Like sacred relic, unprofaned,
  By cold, or common, eye :
And often, shall my pilgrim thoughts,
  Frequent that hallowed shrine,
For hallowed, must I deem the spot,
  That harbours aught of thine.

Thither, shall fond affection, oft,
  Her choicest offerings bring ;
And ardent Hope, oft linger there,
  To plume her weary wing ;
And thence, her strains be wafted, oft,
  The syren Memory ;
And this, the sweetest of them all,
  "To say, I've thought of thee."

1824.

1825–1828.

TO ———.

WHEN compelled, to rest or rove,
Far away, from her I love,
What shall clear the clouded eye?
The mellow light of memory!
Oh! in such an hour, how dear,
Scenes of other days, appear,
Beaming, ever fair and bright,
In magic memory's golden light.

When the tones, I love to hear,
Fall not, on the charméd ear,
What, their music shall supply?
The gentle voice of memory!
Oh, in moments, such as these,
How each treasured tone will please;
Not a pulse, that is not stirred,
By each dear remembered word.

As along the purpling west,
When the sun has sunk to rest,
Many a lengthening line of light
Lingers still, and charms the sight:
So from thee, where'er I roam,
Beaming memories shall come,
Lighting, with their blessed rays,
To brighter hopes, of better days.

1825.

WHAT IS THAT, MOTHER ?

WHAT is that, Mother ?
                    The lark, my child !
The morn has but just looked out, and smiled ;
When he starts, from his humble, grassy nest,
And is up and away, with the dew on his breast,
And a hymn in his heart, to yon pure, bright sphere,
To warble it out, in his Maker's ear :
        Ever my child, be thy morn's first lays,
        Tuned, like the lark's, to thy Maker's praise.

What is that, Mother ?
                    The dove, my son !
And that low sweet voice, like a widow's moan,
Is flowing out, from her gentle breast,
Constant and pure, by that lonely nest,
As the wave is poured from some crystal urn,
For her distant dear one's quick return :
        Ever, my son, be thou, like the dove,
        In friendship as faithful, as constant in love.

What is that, Mother ?
                    The eagle, boy !
Proudly careering his course of joy,
Firm, on his own mountain vigour, relying,
Breasting the dark storm, the red bolt defying,

11

His wing on the wind, and his eye on the sun,
He swerves not a hair, but bears onward, right on :
    Boy, may the eagle's flight ever be thine,
    Onward, and upward, and true to the line.

What is that, Mother ?
                   The swan, my love !
He is floating down, from his native grove ;
No loved one, now, no nestling, nigh,
He is floating down, by himself, to die ;
Death darkens his eye, and unplumes his wings,
Yet the sweetest song, is the last, he sings.
    Live so, my love, that when death shall come,
    Swanlike and sweet, it may waft thee home !
1825.

LINES ON A SEAL.

The device, a leaf.
The motto, " Je ne change, qu'en mourant."

In bower and garden, rich and rare,
    There's many a cherished flower,
Whose beauty fades, whose fragrance flits,
    Within the flitting hour.
Not so the simple forest leaf,
    Unprized, unnoted lying,
The same, thro' all its little life,
    It changes, but in dying.

Be such, and only such, my friend,
    Once mine, and mine for ever :
And here's a hand, to clasp in thine,
    That shall desert thee, never.
And thou, be such, my gentle love,
    Time, chance, the world, defying ;
And take, 'tis all I have, a heart,
    That changes, but in dying.

1825.

FAREWELL.

FAREWELL ! a little magic word,
Which hath been, and which must be, heard,
So long as change and chance shall be
Entwined, with human destiny :
The varied feelings, who can tell,
That mingle in that word, Farewell !

It breathes of joys ; but they are gone ;
Of peace and love, forever flown ;
Of hopes, so faint, they seem but fears ;
Of griefs, that lie, too deep, for tears ;
Of friends, of loved ones, forced to part,
Hand torn from hand, and heart, from heart.

It breathes of joys, that shall again,
With peace and love, resume their reign ;

Of hopes, beneath whose fervent ray,
Each frost-work grief shall melt away,
Of loved ones, met, no more to part,
Hand clasped in hand, and heart, to heart.

Farewell! there's not a thought of mine,
That does not turn to thee, and thine;
There's not a wish, a hope, a prayer,
But thine, and thou, art whispered there,
The hopes, the fears, oh who can tell,
That mingle, in that word, Farewell!

WILD BIRDS.

WILD birds, wild birds; ye rejoice mine eye,
For ye tell, that the rose-wreathed Spring is nigh;
And your warblings fall, on my charméd ear,
Like the wafted notes, of some happier sphere,
Where all, beneath, around, above,
Is breathing of peace, and joy, and love.

Wild birds! ye come in the year's young prime,
That "greenest spot," on the waste of time,
And when, in the bloom of our summer bowers,
Ye have sported away, the sunny hours;
It is but to lift the light wing, and away,
To a milder clime, and a brighter day.

So from the clouds of earth, and time,
Be it ours, to pass to that better clime,
Where night never gathers, and storms never blight,
For God, and the Lamb, are its joy and light.
Who, from that bosom of boundless bliss,
Would return, wild birds ! to a world like this ?

————

DIRGE.

To the beloved memory of my friend and Brother,
the Rev. Cornelius R. Duffie.

Thou art gone from us, my brother ; there is dust upon thy
    brow,
And coldness, in that kindly heart, which ne'er was cold,
    till now ;
And sweet and undisturbed, thy sleep, beneath that chancel
    stone,
Where pious hands, thy couch, have spread ; and thou art
    left alone.

Thou art taken from us, brother ; all thy cares, and labours,
    done,
When, to our short-reaching vision, they had seemed, but
    just begun ;
And long before its noon was reached, thy heaven-enkindled
    ray,
Was lost as stars, by sunlight fade, in cloudless, endless day.

Thou art torn from us, my brother; and our hearts are
    bleeding still,
Yet, taught by thee, in silence, bow to Heaven's all-right-
    eous will,
And bless the grace, which, to thy life, such heavenly ra-
    diance, gave,
To cheer us, while on earth we walk, and light us through
    the grave.

Thou art gone before us, brother; yet we have no tears to
    shed,
For we know, that thou art numbered, with the blessed, holy
    dead;
And in that "continuing city," to which we *may* never come,
Hast found, through faith in Christ our Lord, a welcome
    and a home!
1827.

EARLY PIETY.

"The first fruits—shalt thou give Him."

Young and happy, while thou art,
    Not a furrow, on thy brow,
Not a sorrow, in thy heart,
    Seek the Lord, thy Maker, now!
In its freshness, bring the flower,
    While the dew, upon it, lies;
In the cool and cloudless hour,
    Of the morning sacrifice.

Life will have its evil years ;
  When its skies are overcast,
All the present, thronged with fears,
  And, with vain regrets, the past ;
Let him tremble, who, his heart
  In an hour like this, would bring,
Lest Jehovah say,—" depart !
  'Tis a worn, and worthless thing."

As the first fruits of the year
  Have been chosen of the Lord,
So the first fruits of the heart,
  On His altar, should be poured :
Thus, the blessing, from above
  On life's harvest, shall be given ;
Sown in tears, perhaps on earth,
  Reaped, in joyfulness, in Heaven !

Sept. 1827.

THE TWO ADVENTS.

He came not, with His heavenly crown, His sceptre clad
    with power,
His coming, was in feebleness, the infant of an hour ;
An humble manger cradled, first, the Virgin's holy birth,
And lowing herds companioned there, the Lord of heaven
    and earth.

He came not, in His robe of wrath, with arm outstretched
    to slay;
But, on the darkling paths of earth, to pour celestial day,
To guide in peace, the wandering feet; the broken heart,
    to bind;
And bear, upon the painful cross, the sins of human kind.

And Thou hast borne them, Saviour meek! and therefore,
    unto Thee,
In humbleness, and gratitude, our hearts shall offered be;
And greenly, as the festal bough, that, on Thy altar, lies,
Our souls, our bodies, all be Thine, a living sacrifice!

[1] Yet once again, Thy sign shall be, upon the heavens, dis-
    played,
And earth, and its inhabitants, be terribly afraid,
For, not in weakness, clad, Thou com'st, our woes, our
    sins, to bear,
But girt with all Thy Father's might, His vengeance to
    declare.

The terrors of that awful day, Oh! who shall understand?
Or, who abide, when Thou in wrath, shalt lift Thy holy
    hand?
The earth shall quake, the sea shall roar, the sun in heaven
    grow pale,
But Thou hast sworn, and wilt not change, Thy faithful
    shall not fail!

---

[1] Inserted among the hymns in the present Hymnal.

Then grant us, Saviour! so to pass our time, in trembling,
    here,
That when, upon the clouds of heaven, Thy glory shall
    appear,
Uplifting high our joyful heads, in triumph, we may rise,
And enter, with Thine angel train, Thy temple, in the skies!

Dec. 1827.

THE RAISING OF LAZARUS.

There was a voice of wailing
    In Bethany, that day;
And darkly on that mournful home,
    The cloud of sorrow lay:
And deeply was the fount of grief
    In woman's bosom stirred;
And thickly fell its bitter drops,
    In each low-murmured word.

For never, from that blessed source,
    Of perfectness above,
Was shed on earth, a purer joy,
    Than in a sister's love;
And never pours the bursting heart,
·   A deeper, darker flow,
Than, o'er a brother's wasted form,
    A sister's sacred woe.

12

There was a voice of joyfulness,
  In Bethany, that day,
And brightly, on that happy home,
  The sun of gladness lay;
And deeply was the fount of joy
  In woman's bosom, stirred,
And fervent rose its grateful praise,
  In each exulting word.

For purer, fuller, holier stream,
  Than, in a sister's love,
Flowed never, from that blessed fount,
  Of perfectness, above;
And deeper, warmer, gushing tears,
  On earth, were never shed,
Than fell, that day, upon his neck,
  The rescued from the dead.

Oh, ever thus, on those who love,
  And humbly serve, the Lord,
His blessings, and His chastisements,
  In mingled stream, are poured:
His chastisements, to bring to earth,
  Each thought and purpose high;
His blessings, to lift up our hearts,
  To Him, above the sky.

Then who, whate'er betide, will doubt,
  That all-disposing arm,
Which guides our feet to every good,
  And guards, from every harm?

Since sorrow, like that darkest hour,
 That just precedes the day,
Is only sent, to fit our hearts,
 For joy's unclouded ray.
1828.

LINES ON A SEAL.

The device.— A Sunflower.
The motto — " Je vous suis, partout."

I FOLLOW thee, always,
 By night, and by day ;
Tho' rude, be the weather,
 And rugged, the way ;
Thro' field, and thro' forest,
 My heart is with thee ;
Nor mountain, nor fountain
 Can keep thee, from me.

The sunflower thus,
 To her bright idol, turns,
But turns to him only,
 While brightly he burns ;
And the shadow, that follows,
 All day in the sun,
Will linger, no longer,
 When daylight is gone.

The clouds may come o'er thee,
    In sorrow's dark hour,
But my spirit unshrinking,
    Above them shall tower ;
On wings, as of eagles,
    Exultingly rise,
And play, in the ray,
    Of thy love-speaking eyes.

And tho' grief should encompass thee
    Round, like the night,
Still, my love shall be with thee,
    Thy joy and thy light ;
Nor leave thee, thou dear one,
    Till, lost in the gloom,
Of that blackness of darkness,
    Which broods o'er the tomb.

1828.

———

"THE DEAD IN CHRIST."

Lift not thou the wailing voice ;
    Weep not, 'tis a Christian dieth ;
Up, where blessed saints rejoice,
    Ransomed now, the spirit flieth ;
    High in heaven's own light, she dwelleth,
    Full, the song of triumph swelleth ;

Freed from earth, and earthly failing,
Lift for her, no voice of wailing.

Pour not thou, the bitter tear ;
   Heaven, its book of comfort, opeth ;
Bids thee sorrow not, nor fear,
   But as one, who always hopeth :
Humbly, here, in faith relying,
Peacefully, in Jesus dying,
Heavenly joy, her eye is flushing :
Why should thine, with tears, be gushing ?

They, who die in Christ, are blest ;
   Ours, then, be no thought of grieving ;
Sweetly, with their God, they rest,
   All their toils, and troubles, leaving :
So, be ours, the faith that saveth,
Hope, that every trial, braveth,
Love, that to the end endureth,
And, through Christ, the crown secureth.

1830.

TO ONE "BROKEN IN HEART."

Broken-hearted, weep no more !
   Hear what comfort, He hath spoken,
Smoking flax, who ne'er hath quenched,
   Bruiséd reed, who ne'er hath broken,—

" Ye who wander here below,
" Heavy laden, as you go,
" Come, with grief, with sin, oppressed,
" Come to me, and be at rest."

Lamb of Jesu's blood-bought flock,
    Brought again, from sin and straying,
Hear the Shepherd's gentle voice,—
    'Tis a true and faithful saying ;—
        " Greater love, how can there be,
        " Than to yield up life, for thee ?
        " Bought with pang, and tear, and sigh,
        " Turn and live ! why will ye die ?"

Broken-hearted, weep no more !
    Far, from consolation, flying :
He, who calls, hath felt thy wound,
    Seen thy weeping, heard thy sighing ;
        " Bring thy broken heart, to me,
        " Welcome offering, it shall be,
        " Streaming tears, and bursting sighs ;
        " Mine accepted sacrifice !"

TO A DEAR ONE IN DEEP SORROW.

Dove, whom the Lord hath wounded,
    Return to him, and live ;
For He, alone, who aimed the shaft,
    The remedy, can give.

Dove, whom the Lord hath wounded,
　The bolt was sped in love;
To win thee, from earth's fleeting scenes,
　To better things, above.

Dove, whom the Lord hath wounded,
　He bares for thee, His breast,
And bids thee enter in, and be,
　For evermore, at rest.

Dove, whom the Lord hath wounded,
　Yet waiteth to revive,
Return to Him!—He wounds and heals,
　He kills, and makes alive.

Dove, whom the Lord hath wounded,
　Break through all dull delay:
His strength will bear thy pinions up,
　His goodness, guide thy way.

Dove, whom the Lord hath wounded,
　Though soiled, with sorrows, here,
With silver wings, and plumes of gold,
　In heaven, thou shalt appear.

Dove, whom the Lord hath wounded,
　No more, let earth delay,
But onward, upward, be our flight,
　To realms, of cloudless day!

A CHERUB.

"Are they not all ministering spirits, sent forth to minister to them that shall
be heirs of salvation ?"

BEAUTIFUL thing, with thine eye of light,
And thy brow, of cloudless beauty bright,
Gazing for aye, on the sapphire throne,
Of Him, who dwelleth in light, alone ;
Art thou hasting now, on that golden wing,[1]
With the burning seraph choir, to sing ?
Or stooping to earth, in thy gentleness,
Our darkling path, to cheer and bless ?

Beautiful thing ! thou art come, in love,
With gentle gales, from that world above ;
Breathing of pureness, breathing of bliss,
Bearing our spirits, away from this,
To the better thoughts, to the brighter skies,
Where heaven's unclouded sunshine lies :
Winning our hearts, by a blessed guile,
With that infant look, and angel smile.

Beautiful thing ! thou art come in joy,
With the look, with the voice, of our darling boy,

[1] Yet far more faire, be those bright Cherubins
Which all with *golden wings*, are overdight,
And those eternall *burning Seraphins*,
Which, from their faces, dart out fierie light."
Spenser — Hymne of Heavenly Beautie.

Him that was torn, from the bleeding hearts
He had twined about, with his infant arts,
To dwell, from sin and sorrow far,
In the golden orb, of his little star —[1]
There he rejoiceth, while we, oh ! we,
Long to be happy, and safe, as he.

Beautiful thing ! thou art come in peace,
Bidding our doubts and fears to cease,
Wiping the tears, that, unbidden, start,
From their fountain deep, in the broken heart ;
Cheering us still, on our lonely way,
Lest our hearts should faint, or our feet should stray,
Till, crowned for the conquest, at last we shall be,
Beautiful thing, with our boy, and thee !
Boston, 1828.

THE CLOUD BRIDGE.

SAW ye that cloud which arose in the west,
As the burning sun sank down to rest,
How it spread so wide, and towered so high,
On the molten gold, of that glowing sky,

[1] " Dear Sir,— I am in some little disorder by reason of the death of a little child of mine, a boy that lately made us very glad; but *now he rejoices in his little orbe, while* we thinke, and sigh, and *long to be as safe as he is.*"
Jer. Taylor to Evelyn, July 19, 1656.
" Remember, sir, your two boys are two bright starres, and their innocence is secured, and you shall never hear evil of them agayne."
Jer. Taylor to Evelyn, Feb. 17, 1657.

That it seemed, oh it seemed, like some archéd way,
As it beamed and gleamed, in that glorious ray,
> Where the spirit freed,
> From its earthly weed,
> And robed, in the white,
> Of the saints in light,
Might pass, from the realms of sin and woe,
To that world, where ceaseless pleasures flow.

Ye saw that cloud ; how it towered alone,
Like an archéd path, o'er the billows thrown ;
How its pillars of purple and azure, stood
And mocked at the dash of the angry flood ;
While it beamed, oh it beamed, from its battlements high,
As it gleamed and streamed, in that western sky,
Such a flood of mellow and golden light,
As charmed and fixed, the ravished sight,
And shed, on earth's benighted way,
The peace and joy, of celestial day.

Such, as we haste to our better home,
Saviour, such, be the sights that come;
Thus, while the visions of time flit by,
And the fashion of earth, grows dim to our eye,
Then let the light, oh the light, of Thy love,
Beam bright, on our sight, from the mansions above,
> Rending the gloom,
> That enwraps the tomb,
> And guiding our eye,
> To that world on high,
Where the people that love Thee, forever shall share,
The rest, Thou hast purchased, and gone to prepare.

THE BLESSED SUN WILL SHINE.

"Tis cloudy now. *Sing while the clouds are thick.*
THE BLESSED SUN WILL SHINE !"

" SING, while the clouds are thick,
  " The blessed Sun *will* shine ;"
Far up above the lowering sky
  He pours his flood divine :
· Careering thence, the mighty wave
  Will urge its onward way,
And o'er the loneliest spot of earth
  Pour heaven's benignant ray.

" SING, while the clouds are thick,
  " The blessed Sun *will* shine ;"
The God who hears the infant's cry,
  Will surely answer thine :
· Before the beaming of His smile,
  All forms of sorrow pass,
Like summer clouds, that float at noon,
  Athwart the waving grass.

" SING, while the clouds are thick,
  " The blessed Sun *will* shine ;"
A few short years, and from the sky
  Beams forth the Saviour's sign :
Above the brightness of the Sun,
  It flames, with living light ;
And heaven and earth, through endless days,
  Their songs of joy, unite.

HYMN.

For the Fatherless and Widows' Society.

God of Grace, in glory reigning,
  Far above the eternal sky,
Hear the orphan's sad complaining,
  See the widow's tearful eye.
Thou, all strength and power, possessing,
  Health and comfort, canst impart,
Crown the orphan's cup, with blessing,
  Fill with joy, the widow's heart.

Lord, they were thine own possession,
  In that old Mosaic day,
When, to Judah's favoured nation,
  Thus, thou bad'st, the prophet say ;
" When the ripened harvest, brought in,
  " Fills thy barns, with golden grain,
" Seek not thou, the sheaf forgotten ;
  " 'Tis the homeless stranger's gain !

" When thine olive yields its treasure,
  " Search not every bough, with care ;
God will give thee fuller measure,
  " If thou leave the orphan's share !
" When the land, with purple staining,
  " Thou shalt bring thy vintage, in,
" Grudge not, then, the grapes remaining;
  " Which the widow's hand may glean !"

Lord, whose mercy never changes,
   Whose uprightness, still is sure,
Still the widow's cause avenges,
   Helps the fatherless and poor,
Now, Thine Holy Ghost, outsending,
   From Thy glorious throne, above ;
Fill the hearts, before Thee bending,
   With Thine own exulting love !

THE DILEMMA.

I'VE tried, in much bewilderment, to find,
   Under which phase of loveliness, in thee,
I love thee best ; but, oh, my wandering mind,
   Hovers o'er many sweets, as doth a bee,
     And all I feel, is contradictory.

I love to see thee gay ; because thy smile,
   Is sweeter than the sweetest thing I know ;
And, then, thy limpid eyes, are all the while,
   Sparkling and dancing ; and thy fair cheeks glow,
     With such a sunset lustre, that e'en so,
       I love to see thee gay.

I love to see thee sad ; for then, thy face
   Expresseth an angelic misery ;
Thy tears are shed, with such a gentle grace ;
   Thy words fall soft, yet sweet as words can be,

That, though 'tis selfish, I confess, in me,
I love to see thee sad.

I love to hear thee speak, because thy voice,
Than music's self, is still more musical,
Its tones make every living thing rejoice;
And I, when, on mine ear those accents fall,
In sooth, I do believe, that, most of all,
I love to hear thee speak.

Yet, no! I love thee mute; for, then, thine eyes
Express so much, thou hast no need of speech,
And there's a language, that in silence lies,
When two full hearts look fondness, each to each,
Love's language, that I fain to thee, would teach,
And so, I love thee mute.

Thus, I have come to the conclusion sweet,
Nothing thou dost, can less than perfect be;
All beauties and all virtues, in thee meet;
Yet one thing more, I'd fain behold in thee,
A little love, a little love, for me.

LINES BY THE LAKE-SIDE.

This placid lake, my gentle girl,
Be emblem of thy life,
As full of peace, and purity,
As free from care and strife;

No ripple, on its tranquil breast,
 That dies not, with the day;
No pebble, in its darkest depths,
 But quivers in its ray.

And see, how every glorious form,
 And pageant of the skies,
Reflected, from its glassy face,
 A mirrored image lies;
So be thy spirit, ever pure,
 To God, to virtue, given;
And thought, and word, and action, bear
 The imagery of Heaven.

1831.

1830—1840.

BISHOP RAVENSCROFT.

THE good old man is gone!
He lies in his saintly rest,
 And his labours all are done,
And the work, that he loved the best:
 The good old man is gone,
But the dead, in the Lord, are blessed!

I stood in the holy aisle,
When he spake the solemn word,
 That bound him, through care and toil,
The servant of the Lord:

And I saw, how the depths of his manly soul,
By that sacred vow, were stirred.

And nobly, his pledge he kept ;
For the truth, he stood alone,
And his spirit never slept,
And his march was ever, on !
Oh ! deeply and long, shall his loss be wept;
The brave old man, that's gone.

There were heralds of the cross,
By his bed of death, that stood,
And heard, how he counted all but loss,
For the gain of his Saviour's blood ;
And patiently waited his Master's voice,
Let it call him, when it would.

The good old man is gone !
An apostle's chair is void,
There's dust on his mitre, thrown,
And they've broken his pastoral rod !
And the fold of his love, he has left alone,
To account for its care, to God.

The wise old man is gone ;
His honoured head lies low,
And his thoughts, of power are done,
And his voice's manly flow,
And his pen, that, for truth, like a sword,
            was drawn,
Is still, and soulless, now.

The brave old man is gone !
With his armour on, he fell ;
    Nor a groan, nor a sigh, was drawn,
When his spirit fled, to tell ;
    For mortal sufferings, keen and long,
Had no power, his heart to quell.

The good old man is gone !
He is gone, to his saintly rest ;
    Where no sorrow can be known,
And no trouble can molest ;
    For his crown of life is won,
And the dead, in Christ, are blessed !

Boston, March 15, 1830.

WRITTEN ON LEAVING HOME.

I LEAVE thee, dearest, for a while,
    Yet leave thee, with our God ;
His sheltering wing, is o'er us still,
    At home, and when abroad.

I leave with thee, our little ones,
    The lovely, and the loved ;
And if, for only joy I sought,
    My feet had never roved.

14

But He who gave, and guards them, still,
  Has called me, as His own,
To bear His word to sinful men,
  And lead them to His throne.

Thus must the Master's work be mine,
  Till life's brief hour, is o'er ;
I dare not " love thee," dear, so well,
  Loved I not Jesus, more.

TO MY DEAR GEORGE HOBART.

My beauty and my blessing,
  A year ago, to-day,
Thy little eyes first opened,
  To the morning's blessed ray ;
And, as I saw thee lying,
  On thy gentle Mother's breast,
I felt, what only Fathers feel,
  And cannot be expressed.

My beauty, what strange wonders,
  Since that day, have been wrought ;
Thy life, how wreathed with sunny smiles,
  Thine eye, how full of thought !
How many a queer and quaint device,
  How many a guileless art ;
Thine infant nature's eloquence,
  To win a parent's heart.

My blessing, such I feel thee,
  With each returning day,
A fountain, heaven-opened,
  To refresh life's dusty way ;
To cheer, with love, and hope, the path,
  Else, ah ! how lonely trod,
And lift the heart's affections, up,
  In prayers, for thee, to God.

My beauty and my blessing,
  For thee, my prayers shall rise,
With morning's dawn, and evening's fall,
  Unfailing, to the skies ;
That He, who gave thee, to us,
  Would guard and guide thy way,
Through life, in peace and purity,
  To Heaven's eternal day.

THE FOUNTAIN OPENED IN THE CHURCH.

WITHIN the Church, a fountain springs ;
  It started from the Saviour's side ;
Peace, pardon, joy, to all, it brings,—
  The life-blood of the Crucified.

Its living streams, forever flow,
  Forever pure, forever free ;
The spirit's solace, here below,
  Its succour, for eternity.

" Ho, every one that thirsts, draw nigh — "
    Belovéd, hear the voice divine !
The broken heart, the contrite sigh,
    Are welcome there ; and these are thine.

Come, then — the Spirit calls, — come near,
    In humble faith, in trembling love :
Drink comfort, for thy sorrows here,
    And taste, before, the bliss above.

SPIRIT OF SPRING.

Spirit, that from the breathing south,
    Art wafted hither, on dewy wing,
        By the softened light, of that sunny eye,
        And that voice, of wild-wood melody,
        And those golden tresses, wantoning,
And the perfumed breath, of that balmy mouth,
        We know thee, Spirit of Spring,
Spirit of beauty, these thy charms, Spirit of Spring.

Spirit of Spring, thou comest to wake.
    The slumbering energies of earth,
        The zephyr's breath, to thee, we owe,
        Thine is the streamlet's silver flow,
        And thine, the gentle floweret's birth ;
And their silence, hark ! the wild birds break,
        For thy welcome, Spirit of Spring.

Spirit of Spring, when the cheek is pale,
  There is health, in thy balmy air,
    And peace, in that brow of beaming bright,
    And joy, in that eye of sunny light;
  And golden hope, in that flowing hair;
Oh ! that such influence e'er should fail,
    For a moment, Spirit of Spring,   .
· Spirit of health, peace, joy, and hope; Spirit of Spring.

Yet fail it must, for it comes of earth,
And it may not shame its place of birth,
Where the best can bloom, but a single day,
And the fairest, is first to fade away.

But oh ! there's a changeless world above,
A world of peace, and joy, and love,
    Where, gathered from the tomb,
The holy hopes, that earth hast crost,
And the friends, so dear, we have loved and lost,
    Shall enjoy immortal bloom.

Who will not watch, and strive, and pray,
That his longing soul may soar away,
    On faith's untiring wing,
To join the throng of saints in light,
In that world, forever fair and bright,
    Of endless, cloudless, Spring.

1833.

THE AMULET OF GRACE.

Written in "the Amulet."

DEAREST, could thy husband get,
With his blood, an amulet,
That could charm away thy woe,
From his heart the stream should flow.

But from mortal misery,
Such redemption may not be;
Vain before the holy God,
Oceans filled with human blood.

Yet let heaven and earth resound,
Such a ransom has been found,
God's atoning Lamb has died,
Jesus has been crucified.

Dearest, let that fountain be,
Opened, not in vain, for thee:
It alone, can soothe, can save;
Seek, by faith, its precious wave.

Seek it, sweet one, while you may,
Seek it, while 'tis called to day.
Seek the Lamb, for sinners slain—
None who seek Him, seek in vain.

January 1, 1833.

TO MY DEAR SISTER.

My sister, I remember,
  How lonely was my heart,
Till thou, in all its joys and griefs,
  Wert born, to bear a part :—
And well do I remember
  The pleasure and the pride,
That filled my boyish bosom,
  When thou wert by my side.

My sister, since you joined me,
  Upon life's rugged way,
Through what vicissitudes, we've passed,
  Of darkness and of day.
Yet still, thy love has steadfast been,
  Unchanged in cloud, or shine,
And thy own sorrow, been forgot,
  To sympathize with mine.

My sister, to repay thee
  Is only, with the Lord,
And He can make thy love, its own
  Exceeding great reward.
O ! ever may His sheltering shield,
  Outstretched above thee, lie,
And brightest beams of light, direct
  Thy footsteps, to the sky.

Philadelphia, March 2, 1834.

TO WILLIAM CROSWELL.

" Perennis et Fragrans."

WILLIAM, my brother and my bosom friend !
　　For thrice ten years, the sun, this blessed day,
　　Has lighted thee along life's chequered way,
Serene and placid, towards thy journey's end.
One third the distance, we have trod together,
　　Hand grasping hand, and heart enclosed in heart,
　　Each of the other's life, breath, being, part ;
Breasting as one, time's rough and rugged weather.
　　Poet and Priest, as in thy face I look,
　　So full of thought, so tranquil, so benign,
　　With pride of soul, to hail thee friend of mine,
I greet thee, with the legend of this book :—
" Fragrant and lasting," be thy memory here,
And then a fadeless crown, through heaven's immortal
　　　　year !

Burlington, Nov. 7, 1834.

A PRAYER.

GRANT me, great Lord, Thy graces three,
Faith, and Hope, and Charity ;
Faith, that on the cross relies,
And trusts, but in Thy sacrifice.

Hope, that, when by woe opprest,
Points upward to a heavenly rest;
And last, the greatest of the three,
O ! give me gentle Charity:
To suffer all; to know no pride;
To strive, another's faults to hide;
To answer with a soothing smile,
When men, with angry words, revile;
To envy not that happiness,
Thy hand denies me, to possess;
The rich man's wealth to covet not,
Though poverty should be my lot.
Teach me through every earthly ill,
To be submissive, to Thy will;
And let me of Thy grace, receive,
As I, my enemies, forgive,
Then Faith, and Hope, and Charity
Will lead me on, to Heaven, through Thee.

THE GERANIUM LEAF.

"It grew and blew, in my little room, and I pressed it in my Bible."

TEN thousand thanks, my dearest, for this precious little
    leaf,
Henceforth, to bear me company, in pleasure and in grief;
Still breathing to my heart, its fragrant memories of thee,
And consecrating all the past, with natural piety.

15

I gaze upon its greenness, and I think of where it blew,
Till all that charméd atmosphere grows radiant to my view,
And I felt it was a happy lot, to live, and grow, and bloom,
Beneath thy light of loveliness, in that enchanted room.

Be ever thus, my gentle one, the Bible at thy side,
And every joy and every grief, shall thus be sanctified ;
Nor trust the love, that only drinks at fountains of the earth,
To satisfy the longings, of a soul of heavenly birth.

    1838.

SPRING THOUGHTS.

DEAREST, those purple flowers,
   They seem to me to spring,
From the grave of him,[1] whose loving breast
Was wont to be the living nest
   Of each beautiful thought and thing.

Dearest, those early flowers,
   They speak to me of him,
With the youthful mind, so richly stored
With loftiest thoughts, and as freely poured,
   As from fountain's bubbling brim.

Dearest, those fragrant flowers
   Are odours of his life,

[1] The Rev. B. D. Winslow.

The gentle-hearted, the heavenly-willed,
With the choicest grace of the Holiest, filled,
    Where loveliest deeds, were rife.

Dearest, they breathe, those flowers,
    Of the land, where he takes his rest,
Where the river of immortality flows,
With our White, and Hobart, and Jebb, and Rose,
    And all, that he loved, the best.

Dearest, they say, those flowers —
    Earth's winter womb's first born —
" So shall the dead in Christ arise,
Heirs of the world, beyond the skies,
    On the resurrection morn."

1839.

––––––––

TO MY WIFE.

" It is well." [1]

BELOVED, " it is well !—"
    God's ways are always right ;
And love is o'er them all,
    Though far above our sight.

[1] In a little book of Dr. Bedell's, having this title.

Beloved, " it is well !— "
　　Though deep and sore, the smart,
　He wounds, who skills to bind,
　　And heal the broken heart.

Beloved, " it is well ! — "
　　Though sorrow clouds our way,
　'Twill make the joy more dear,
　　That ushers in the day.

Beloved, " It is well !— "
　　The path that Jesus trod,
　Though rough and dark it be,
　　Leads home, to heaven, and God.

March 2, 1833.

―――――――

TO MY WIFE.

My only, and my own one,
　　How dark and drear, the day
That drags its lingering hours along ;
　　When thou art far away,
The loveliness, that lighted up
　　My life, no longer nigh,
And hushed the voice, that used to fill
　　My soul with melody.

High, in the broad blue firmament,
   Among those worlds of light,
The faithful witness holds her place,
   Constant, serene, and bright ;
My aching heart in sadness sinks,
   For so, her placid eye
Looked down, when heart to heart, we walked,
   In hours of joy, gone by.

I sit among my silent books,
   And think, with what a pride,
I scanned their hoarded treasures o'er,
   When thou wert by my side ;
I listen for thy gentle step,
   I watch the opening door;
The page is marked, the pen laid down,
   Alas ! thou comest no more.

By day or night ; at home, abroad,
   Where'er I roam or rest,
The thought of thee, my absent love,
   Thus fills my faithful breast ;
Nor bitter, bitter, though it be,
   As pang of parting life ;
Has earth a joy, my soul so craves,
   While thou'rt away, my wife.

TO MY DEAR SISTER.

ON HER 19TH BIRTHDAY,

My gentle sister, if the love,
  My bosom bears for thee,
Were poured, like running waters, out,
  'Twould be a surging sea.
But fullest streams, are ever those,
  Most silently which run,
And the deep earth has deeper founts,
  Than ever see the sun.

My gentle sister, could the thoughts,   .
  That throng my heart, of thee,
Be coined in ducats, what a shower,
  Of minted gold, 'twould be !
But richest ores, lie farthest down,
  And, ripening in the mine,
Sleep gold and jewels, costlier far
  Than all, on earth, that shine.

Then, gentle sister, think not hard,
  Nor count it, loss of love,
That ne'er for thee, in idle hours,
  One idle rhyme I've wove ;
That fitful harp, whose sleeping strings,
  The wild wind wakes at will,
The soul of music harbours yet,
  Though all its strings are still.

Then, sister dearest, with the year,
  That newly dawns to-day,
To light thee on, in gentlenesss,
  Thy pure and peaceful way ;
Take deeply, warmly, from the heart,
  The silent prayer of love —
God's blessing be thy portion here,
  His blessedness above !

TO MY DEAR SISTER.

My gentle sister, twenty years,
  To day, have flitted by,
Since first thou camest, a helpless thing,
  Among our hearts to lie.
We welcomed thee, as best we might,
  With mingled smiles and tears;
And poured, we could no more, our prayers,
  For blessings on thy years.

And, sister sweet, our prayers were heard,
  God's blessed one thou art :
Not, with the rich, or proud, or gay,
  But, with the pure in heart :
His gifts, to thee, in gentleness
  And piety, are given ;
The treasures that endure, on earth,
  And never fail in heaven,

My gentle sister, thou hast been,
  Even as a child to me,
Since first thy new-born helplessness
  Was tended on my knee ;
And stretched upon the shaded bank,
  Whole summer days, I lay,
And watched, as with a parent's joy,
  Thy happy, infant play.

And still, the holy bond endures,
  And still, a father's care
Makes tenderer, deeper, more intense,
  The love, for thee, I bear.
It grows with years, with cares it grows,
  Unchanged by change of lot ;
In joy and sorrow, hope and fear,
  Still failing, faltering not.

My gentle sister may the years,
  That yet remain to thee,
Be spent, as all the past have been,
  In tranquil piety :
May Heaven, in mercy, spare thee long
  To all who share thy love ;
And faith and peace, prepare thee here,
  For endless joy above !

1840–1850.

TO MY TWO DEAR CHILDREN.

CORNELIA AND ANNIE R.

YOUR beautiful present,[1] my children,
 Has filled me with pleasure and joy,
That the thought of my personal comfort,
 Your fingers, and hearts, should employ.
Be assured of my fond supplication,
 That you, in all grace may increase,
And *your feet* have that blest " preparation "
 That comes from the " Gospel of Peace."

Christmas, 1846.

THE SMELL OF SPRING.

The first violets of the year 1840, seen this day, 4th March, Ash Wednesday.

THE smell of Spring ! how it comes to us,
 In those simple, wild-wood flowers,
With memories sweet, of friends and home,
When never a cloud on our sky had come,
 In childhood's cheerful hours.

[1] A pair of slippers.

16

The smell of Spring ! how it comes to us,
  In that cluster of purple bloom,
With thoughts of the loved and loving one,
Not lost, we know, but before us gone,
  Whom we left, in his wintry tomb.

The smell of Spring ! how it comes to us,
  In the violet's fragrant breath,
With beaming hopes of that brighter shore,
Where flowers and friends, shall fall no more,
  " And there shall be no more death."
1840.

TO A DEAR LITTLE BOY.

WITH A BIBLE.

THIS little book, my precious boy,
  If studied and obeyed,
Will bring Heaven's choicest blessings down
  Upon thy youthful head ;

Will lead thee, shouldst thou grow a man,
  Safe through life's pilgrimage ;
And crown thy latest days with peace,
  The glory of old age.

Nay, will not leave thee then, my boy,
    But through the darkling grave
Support and guide thy shrinking feet,
    And in the judgment, save.

Then take this book, my precious boy,
    And study it with prayer ;
'Twill charm for thee each ill of earth,
    And foil each secret snare.

'Twill teach thee, wisely, how to live,
    And, better, how to die ;
And bring thee, saved, through Christ, from sin,
    To reign with Him, on high.

WITH A BIBLE AND PRAYER BOOK,

TO MY GODSON.

DEAR boy, had I the wealth of worlds
    To lavish full and free,
I could add nothing to the gifts,
    Which now I send to thee.

The Word of God, the Church's prayers
    With all thy heart embrace ;
And thou shalt never lose the gift,
    Of thy baptismal grace.

The cross, imprinted on thy brow,
    Enthronéd thus within,
Shall save thee from the guilt and power,
    And punishment of sin ;

Through all the changing scenes of life
    Thy succour and thy stay,
Shall guide thee onward thro' the grave,
    To realms of endless day.

ON THE LITTLE URN IN THE GARDEN.

"H. T. *Jan.* 16, 1815. M. T. *Oct.* 12, 1815."

"Lovely and pleasant in their lives, and in their death they were not divided."

WIND, graceful clematis, around the urn,
    Where filial love, a Mother's name has traced,
Type of her loveliness, whose loss we mourn,
    With every charm, with every virtue, graced.

Wave, tall acacia, o'er the sacred stone,
    Which bears inscribed a Father's honoured name ;
So was his sheltering shadow, round us, thrown,
    So fresh, so full, the verdure of his fame.

Blend thus your leaf and tendril, vine and tree,
    And waft, as one, the fragrance of your flowers ;
So they, in fond communion, full and free,
    Passed their sweet lives, amid these happy bowers.

Sweet sainted ones, thus lovely in your life,
 Nor, in your peaceful death, divided long,
Saved from the world, its sin, its care, its strife,
 May we but join you, in that white-robed throng.
Battersea Rise, 1841.

"SO HE GIVETH HIS BELOVED SLEEP."

" Your boy is looking as peaceful and happy, asleep in his cradle,
as you can desire."

SLEEP lies like dew about thee,
 The sleep, which God bestows ;
Nor pain, nor care, nor sorrow, yet,
 Thy peaceful spirit knows :
Washed, from the first transgression,
 In that baptismal flood ;
God makes thee, His beloved,
 Through the Beloved's blood.

Sleep sweetly on, and safely,
 Mine own baptismal child ;
Calm, as the stream in Eden's bower,
 While yet Jehovah smiled ;
The heavenly Dove hangs o'er thee,
 With blessed, brooding wing,
To shelter and to shield thee,
 From evil thought and thing.
London, August 24, 1841.

THE BEAUCHAMP MONUMENT,

IN THE CHOIR OF WARWICK CHURCH.

"Te spectem, suprema mihi cum venerit hora,
Te teneam moriens deficiente manu." [1]

Tibullus Eleg., i. 59, 60.

" LOVE, let me take thy hand,
    That tenderest, truest one,
The same I held, when we did stand,
    Before the altar stone :
There, let me hold it so ;
    It stays my fluttering heart :
Nor, till its pulses cease to flow,
    Permit that grasp to part.

" Nay,— when thy breast, my bride,
    Mingles its dust with mine,
And sweetly sleeping, side by side,
    We rest beneath the shrine ;
So let the Sculptor's art,
    Our love perpetuate :
The grasp, that life could never part,
    Death shall but consecrate !"

[1] Thee let me gaze on, with my dying breath,
And clasp thy hand, when mine relents in death.
                                        G. W. D.

Thus dying Beauchamp spake ;
　　His will was strictly done ;[1]
Sweetly they sleep, as once they stood,
　　Before the altar-stone ;
He, in his mailéd coat,
　　She, in her bridal vest ;
In sculptured beauty, side by side,
　　And hand in hand, they rest.

I've stood among the tombs,
　　In many an ancient fane,
Where mitred head, and sworded hand,
　　Call ages up, again :
But all the stone seems here
　　Instinct with vital breath ;
And this, its lesson to the heart —
　　Love, overmastering death.

Stratford-upon-Avon, 24*th July*, 1841.

---

[1] In the centre of the choir is a fine table monument, supporting the recumbent effigies of Earl Thomas Beauchamp, the founder of the choir, and Catharine, his Countess, daughter of Roger Mortimer, Earl of March. The Earl is represented in armour covered with a surcoat, a dagger on his right side, spurs on his heels, his left hand gauntleted, resting on his sword, *his right hand uncovered, clasping that of his Countess*, his helmeted head supported by a cushion, his feet resting on a bear. His Countess is habited in a mantle and petticoat, laced down the front, below the girdle, and very rich, her sleeves reaching to the wrists, and buttoned, her headdress reticulated, her head supported by a cushion, and her feet resting on a lamb. *Her right hand is clasped in that of the Earl*, her left hand reposes on her breast.

THE BEAUCHAMP MONUMENT.[1]

HAND in hand, we stood together,
   At the altar-stone ;
Hand in hand, in roughest weather,
   Life-long, we have gone :
Hand in hand, in hours of gladness,
   Cheerily we strayed ;
Hand in hand, in hours of sadness,
   Knelt to God, and prayed.

Hand in hand, we went, my own love,
   For a little while ;
Hand in hand, we'll sleep, in stone, love,
   In the sacred aisle :
Hand in hand, the trumpet sounding,
   Saved through Christ, we'll rise ;
Hand in hand, through grace abounding,
   Soar beyond the skies.

The Breakers, 9th June, 1853.

HOC ERAT IN VOTIS.

THIS was in all my prayers, since first I prayed,
A parsonage in a sweet garden's shade ;

[1] This was written twelve years later ; the impression still fresh and strong.

The Church adjoining with its ivied tower;
A peal of bells; a clock to tell the hour;
A rustic flock to feed from day to day;
And kneel with them, at morn and eve, and pray.

He, who doth all things well, denied my prayer,
And bade me take the apostle's staff, and bear;
The scattered sheep, o'er hill and dale, pursue,
Tend the old flocks, and gather in the new;
Count ease, and health, and life, and all things, loss,
So I make known, the blessed, bleeding Cross.

These quiet scenes, that never can be mine,
This home-bred happiness, dear friend, be thine;
Each choicest gift, and influence from above,
Descend on thee, and all that share thy love;
Peace, which the world gives not, nor can destroy,
The prelibation of eternal joy.

Northfield Vicarage, August 3, 1841.

.TO MY DEAR WILLIE,

ON HIS TWELFTH BIRTH-DAY

My second born, my gentle,
  My sweet and precious boy,
Sent to us, in our darkling day,
  To be our bosoms' joy;

17

How like a sunbeam, to our hearts,
　　Thy beauty, in our eyes,
Dispelling every cloud, that spreads
　　Its sackcloth, on the skies.

Be ever thus, my blessing,
　　So patient and so meek ;
So careful always, what to do,
　　So thoughtful what to speak;
Till grown in wisdom, as in years,
　　Through His abounding grace,
He take thee,— 'tis my fondest prayer —
　　To fill a deacon's place.

How sweet, should he permit it,
　　To lean on thy stout arm !
Thy silver-voicéd litany,
　　Mine ear, how it will charm !
And, when my days are numbered all,
　　And all my labours, done ;
My death-bed, with the Church's prayers,
　　Console and cheer, my son !

March 2, 1844.

———

"How often little lucid intervals of the most golden light, fall in upon our
path; as you have seen it, through a trellised vine."

Look, dearest, how the golden glow,
　　Gleams, through the trellised vine ;
Chequering with light and shade, the way,
　　Before thy feet, and mine :

So, on our path of parted life,
    When clouds shut out the day,
Love's lucid intervals fall in,
    As here, the sunbeams play.

And could our linked and loving feet,
    Together, walk through life,
This beating breast, these clasping arms,
    Thy home, my more than wife ;
How would the clouds, about our path,
    Be fleckered with the day ;
And gleams of love's own golden light,
    Chequer life's trellised way !

THE SELF-FLOWING.

"The grapes are collected late in the season, and picked one by one. The juice runs, from its own pressure, over a grooved table, into earthen jars. The quantity is small, and very precious. It is called, *Ausbruch*; the self-flowing."

    SWEETEST, in the Rhine-land,
    Famous, as a vine-land,
When the golden clusters burst with juice,
    They hang them by the stems,
    All gleaming, there, like gems ;
To let the luscious, limpid, liquor loose :
    And these sweet, spontaneous, streams,
    Every Rhinelander still deems,
The choicest, that the vintage can produce.

So my verses, dearest,
 Sprung from love sincerest,
Filling all my spirit, full of thee,
 Gushing out, like fountains,
 Down the side of mountains,
Flow, forever full, and fresh, and free ;
 Or breathe, like scent, from flowers,
 In Spring's first, dewy, hours,
When violets and roses tempt the bee.

TO MY ENGLISH GOD-SON,

JAMES WILLIAM DOANE FORSTER, ON HIS BAPTISMAL DAY.

God's blessing rest upon thee,
 My precious little boy ;
Make thee thy mother's comfort still,
 And still thy father's joy ;
Conduct thee, through life's pilgrimage,
 In purity and peace ;
And take thee, to that blessed world,
 Where sin and sorrow cease.

Long time, I've loved thy father,
 Thy gentle mother, too ;
And tenderest cords, have twined our hearts,
 Across the waters blue ;

And now, I sit beside their hearth,
    An honoured, happy guest,
And feel, how truly Christian home
    Is type of heavenly rest.

Dear child, how opportunely,
    Thy coming has been timed,
And providential orderings,
    With human wishes, chimed ;
That hearts, which long in unison,
    Have.beat, beyond the sea,
Should flow together, at the font,
    And blend themselves, in thee.

Dear child of dearest parents,
    I take thee to my heart,
To be, as they, so long have been,
    Its parcel and its part ;
To grow, like sweetest flower, beside
    That sainted Bishop's [1] tomb.
And give, its sweetest memories,
    New fragrance and new bloom.

Dear child, with Thornton, [2] Forster, Jebb
    My name is knit in thee,
All written in that Blessed Book,
    One Christian family.

[1] Bishop Jebb, "the good Bishop of Limerick." Mr. Forster was his Domestic Chaplain, and his " own familiar friend."

[2] The excellent Henry Thornton, M.P., his maternal grandfather; Miss Isabella Thornton was a god-mother.

So when the dead shall all come forth,
At that clear trumpet's sound,
May each dear name, recorded in
The Lamb's own Book, be found.

Stisted Rectory, August 15, 1841. ·

BATTERSEA RISE.

THE THORNTON FAMILY RESIDENCE, CLAPHAM COMMON.

OLD house, how long I've known thee,
By high, historic fame,
By Thornton, Inglis, Wilberforce,[1]
Each loved and sainted name ;
And now, my pilgrim feet have trod
Thy consecrated ground,
And underneath thy sacred roof,
A pilgrim's rest, have found.

[1] Battersea Rise, Clapham Common, a few miles from London, was the residence of the late Henry Thornton, Esq. M.P. At his death, it became the residence of his friend, and the faithful guardian of his children, Sir R. H. Inglis, Bart., M.P. It is now occupied by the eldest son, Henry Sykes Thornton, Esq., and his family. In this House, Mr. Wilberforce wrote his " Practical View." Sir Robert Inglis' edition of Mr. Thornton's Family Prayers, bears date from this house. It was the resort, besides these, of Hannah More, the Grants, the Bowdlers, Macaulay, Babington. The excellent Dr. Dealtry is the rector of Clapham. The late Rev. Charles Thornton, who translated S. Cyprian's Treatises, for the Library of the Fathers, at Oxford, was the son of Mr. Henry Thornton.

Home of each heart-attraction,
　Of manly piety,
Of lovely woman's gentleness,
　Of childhood's artless glee ;
A tenderer tie, than history, now
　Shall hold thee, to my heart,
And make thy blessed memory,
　Of every pulse, a part.

My children shall be told of thee,
　And every dearest name,
In every murmured orison,
　Their lips, shall learn to frame ;
And fervent prayers, shall daily rise,
　From far beyond the sea,
That God, His blessings, still may pour,
　Sweet Christian home, on thee !

Battersea Rise, August 20, 1841.

MY BEST OF BLESSINGS.

MY best of blessings, when from thee,
　I turn my feet, away,
My heart dies down, as children's do,
　From hearth and home who stray ;
The heart, that fears no face of man,
　Nor shrinks, from shape of ill,
All melted, like a weaned child's,
　Is swayed, at thy sweet will.

Upon the stern and stormy sea,
　When tempests foam and frown,
The gentle moon, serene and still,
　In loveliness, looks down :
Silent and sweet, her tender eye
　The heaving mass controls,
And the whole world of water sleeps,
　Till not a ripple rolls.

My best of blessings, in my heart,
　Subdued, to love and thee,
Thy gentle beauty sinks, as soft
　As moonlight, in the sea :
Its waves and billows heave no more,
　Its storms and tempests cease :
And all its troubled depths are lulled,
　In placidness, and peace.

THE CATHOLIC'S ASSERTION OF THE CROSS.

" God forbid that I should glory, save in the Cross of our Lord Jesus Christ."
Gal. vi. 14.

" We do sign him with the sign of the Cross."— *Baptismal Office.*

Lift up the Cross, lift up the Cross !
　Let it surmount each loftiest spire,
And beam, the beacon of the world,
　To warn it, from eternal fire.

Lift up the Cross, lift up the Cross !
   Let every eye the token see,
And look, through it, to Him, Whose blood
   Streamed, for them, from the atoning Tree.

Lift up the Cross ! Through all the storms
   Of more than eighteen hundred years,
Its changeless beauty, clear and calm,
   The radiant signature uprears ;
Unharmed it stands, undimmed it shines,
   And sheds its glory, near and far ;
God's pillar-light, to guide His Church,
   Salvation's " bright and morning star."

Lift up the Cross ! Rome shall not have
   Our birthright, in that blessed sign :
We still will bear it, on the brow,
   We still will rear it on the shrine.
So that be ours, and we be His,
   All other things, we count " but loss ;"
Our single hope, the Crucified,
   And all our glory, in the Cross.

Riverside, Tuesday in Easter Week, 1843.

TO A MOURNING MOTHER.

MOTHER weep ! the heart is flesh ;
Wounds will bleed while they are fresh ;

18

Gentlest hands, the flower, may crop;
Tears will trickle, drop by drop.

Yet, weep not! that darling child,
Like a bird, as sweet and wild,
Has but winged her winter flight,
To the land of life and light.

There, she builds her blessed nest,
In the gentle Saviour's breast;
While, that flute-like voice, she tries,
In celestial symphonies.

Mothers' tears lie near the lid;
Mothers' tears can not be hid;
This, the thought, to dry their eyes—
One more song, in Paradise!

TO MY HEART.

FROM THE ITALIAN OF SAVONAROLA.

My heart, if thou at peace wilt be,
Thou canst no longer, live with me;
Fly to Jesus, there to stay,
From this false world, far away;
Favour here, can only be,
At the cost of treachery.

While on earth, thou art with me,
Bitter all thy life must be.
Faith and peace, are fled afar;
Everywhere, there is but war.
If thy life is dear to thee,
To the light of Jesus, flee.

COME WHEN THOU WILT.

COME, in the sun-glint, or come, in the shower;
Come, with the snow-flake, or come, with the flower;
Come, when thou wilt, thou art welcome to me,
As the fragrance of Spring, to the scent of the bee.

Come, at the dawn of day, come, at its close;
Come with the violet, come with the rose:
Come when thou wilt, thou art fair, to my eye,
As the first star of evening, that flames from the sky.

Come, at the noon-tide, or come in the night;
Come, when the skies are black, come, when they're bright;
Come, when thou wilt, thou art dear to my heart,
As the streams of red life, from its fountain, that start.

Come, in the Winter, or come, in the Spring;
Come, when the birds are still, come, when they sing;
Come, when thou wilt, and thy coming shall be,
For beauty, for balm, and for blessing, to me.

TO MY WIFE.

WITH AN ILLUSTRATED COPY, OF "THE BABES IN THE WOOD."

DEAR, when you and I were young,
How delightedly, we hung
    On this little story :
Still its simple beauty charms
Every age ; the babe in arms,
    Maids, and matrons hoary.
This the lesson : truth and nature,
    Everywhere, alike prevail ;
Love and beauty are immortal,
    Trust in God can never fail.

Riverside, Eve of the Circumcision, 1848.

GLEAMS OF SUNSHINE IN A DARKENED ROOM.

MORNING.

" Joy cometh in the morning."

O, COME with blessings, new-born day,
    To all, my soul holds dear ;
Or, bring the grace that crowns them all,
    To die without a fear !

NOON.

"Never give up."

"Never give up!"   It can be of no use,
    Tugging and trying, may bring something round again.
Bread, that is cast on the waters, profuse,
    Scripture hath told us, shall surely be found again.

"Never give up!"   We can make nothing by it,
    'Tis but to die, when the breath has gone out from us.
While the last moment lasts, take it, and try it.
    "God for the right!" will dispel every doubt from us.

EVENING.

"Light is sown, for the righteous."

Night closes in : but, to the just,
    The light of God is sown ;
As seeds, upon the furrowed field,
    In opening Spring, are strown.

Through cold, through heat, through calm, through storm,
    It works its steadfast way ;
And, at the harvest-time, breaks forth,
    In floods of golden day.

Riverside, November, 1848.

THE SAILOR'S HOME.

The Floating[1] Church of the Redeemer, for Sailors and Boatmen; built at Bor-
dentown, New Jersey; and to be moored at a wharf in Philadelphia.   The
seats are all to be free.

THE Jersey woods are tall and green,
The Jersey mines are broad and deep,
And cool and pure, the sparkling streams,
That, down the Jersey mountains, leap.

Search out, from all the Jersey woods,
The sturdiest oaks, the loftiest pines ;
And gather in the choicest ore,
That deepest lies, in Jersey mines.

And, where the Jersey mountain streams
Fill the deep rolling Delaware,
Lay, broad and strong, the Christian keel,
And fasten every plank, with prayer.

Complete the sacred structure stands,
And towers, majestic, from the wave :
A floating Church, a Christian ark ;
The sailor's soul, from sin, to save.

Float gently down, thou blessed bark,
To Philadelphia's ship-lined shore ;
And moored 'long side her teeming wharves,
Unfold the Gospel's sacred store.

[1] Now St. John's Church, Camden, N. J.

Show, from the topmast's tallest peak,
The great Redeemer's glorious name;
Display the blessed, bleeding Cross;
Its love, its agony, its shame.

Proclaim the life-restoring Word;
Pour all the energy of prayer;
Sprinkle the blest baptismal wave;
The Bread, the Wine, of life, prepare.

Arrest the thoughtless, check the rash,
Win home the wanderer, from his ways;
The broken-hearted, bind with balm,
And fill the penitent with praise.

Like clouds that scud before the storm,
Like doves that to their windows come;
Crowd, brothers, to the floating Cross,
And find the Church, the Sailor's Home.

Riverside, St. John the Evangelist, 1848.

THE CHILD AT PRAYER.

A CAST FROM GREENOUGH.

CHILD that kneelest meekly there,
Pouring all thy soul in prayer,
Would that I might be like thee,
In unreserving piety!

Such as thou, did Jesus take,
Model for mankind, to make;
Such as thou, in guileless love,
Nursling of the Heavenly Dove.

Oh, that while on thee, I gaze,
I might learn thy blessed ways;
All thy confidence of heart,
All thine innocence of art!

Saviour, once Thyself a child,
Good and gentle, meek and mild,
Make me such as this to be;
Reproduce Thyself, in me!

———

THE BANNER OF THE CROSS.

FLING out the Banner! Let it float,
    Sky-ward, and sea-ward, high and wide;
The sun, that lights its shining folds,
    The Cross, on which, the Saviour died.

Fling out the Banner! Angels bend,
    In anxious silence, o'er the sign;
And vainly seek to comprehend
    The wonder of the love divine.

Fling out the Banner! Heathen lands
   Shall see, from far, the glorious sight,
And nations, crowding to be born,
   Baptize their spirits in its light.

Fling out the Banner! Sin-sick souls,
   That sink and perish in the strife,
Shall touch, in faith, its radiant hem,
   And spring, immortal, into life.

Fling out the Banner! Let it float,
   Sky-ward, and sea-ward, high and wide;
Our glory, only in the Cross;
   Our only hope, the Crucified.

Fling out the Banner! Wide and high,
   Sea-ward and sky-ward, let it shine:
Nor skill, nor might, nor merit, ours;
   We conquer only in that sign.

Riverside, 2d Sunday in Advent, 1848.

WALL FLOWERS.

— "They smell sweetest by night-time, thae flowers; and they're maist aye
seen about ruined buildings. " — Edie Ochiltree, *in the Antiquary.*

Sweetest by night: like gracious words,
   That scent the sacred page;
But freeliest pour their perfumed store,
   In sickness, grief, and age.

19

Seen most by ruins : like the love,
   That gave itself for all ;
Yet closest clings to guiltiest things,
   As Magdalene, or Saul.

Riverside, December, 1848.

———

RASPBERRY VINEGAR, WITH ICED WATER.

IN EXTREME ILLNESS.

BREATH of Summer, how I feel you,
   As you play about my brow ;
Wings of damask roses fan me,
   Through that bed of violets, now.

Smell of blossom ; taste of berry ;
   Sound of brooklet ; flash of bird :
All the memories of my boyhood
   Have, in turn, my bosom stirr'd.

Hand, That holds me ; Eye, That guides me ;
   Heart, That loved me, to the death :
New devotion thrills my spirit,
   While I breathe this summer breath !

Riverside, January 29, 1849.

MALLEUS DOMINI.

"Is not My word, saith the Lord, like a hammer that breaketh the rock in pieces?"— *Jeremiah xxiii*, 29.

Sledge of the Lord, beneath whose stroke,
The rocks are rent, the heart is broke,
I hear thy pond'rous echoes ring,
And fall a crushed and crumbled thing.

Meekly these mercies I implore,
Through Him Whose Cross, our sorrows, bore;
On earth, Thy new-creating grace;
In heaven, the very lowest place.

Oh, might I be a living stone,
Set in the pavement of Thy throne;
For sinner saved, what place so meet,
As, at the Saviour's bleeding feet.

Riverside, September 19, 1849.

AN ANSWER.

You asked me once my dearest,
Why infants ever die,
And when I could not answer
You sweetly, told me why—

That so, in heaven, those loveliest things
Of earth, we might not miss ;
The radiance of an infant's smile,
The fragrance of its kiss.

"SWEET FROM THE RAIN."

"The violets are sweet, from the rain, this morning," my gardener said, "I
let it in upon them."

"SWEET from the rain : " the scentless shower
Upon the earth descends ;
And all Arabia, in the flower,
Its thousand odours, blends.

"Sweet from the rain : " so human hearts
Grow tender, after tears ;
And sorrow, sanctified, imparts
The peace of happier spheres.

"Sweet from the rain : " beloved, so
Thy kindness soothes my heart ;
And joys, I thought no more to know,
Their sympathies impart.

"Sweet from the rain : " the heavenly grace,
On sinful souls, is poured ;
And from the lost and guilty race,
Rise praises, to the Lord.

Στῆϑι ἑδραιος ὡς ἀκμῶν τυπτόμενος.

ST. IGNATIUS TO ST. POLYCARP, BOTH MARTYRS.

" STAND, like an anvil, " when the stroke,
    Of stalwart men, falls fierce and fast ;
Storms, but more deeply, root the oak,
    Whose brawny arms embrace the blast.

" Stand like an anvil, " when the sparks
    Fly far and wide, a fiery shower ;
Virtue and truth must still be marks,
    Where malice proves its want of power.

" Stand like an anvil," when the bar,
    Lies, red and glowing, on its breast ;
Duty shall be life's leading star,
    And conscious innocence, its rest.

" Stand like an anvil," when the sound
    Of pond'rous hammers pains the ear ;
Thine, but the still and stern rebound
    Of the great heart, that cannot fear.

" Stand like an anvil ; " noise and heat
    Are born of earth, and die with time ;
The soul, like God, its source and seat,
    Is solemn, still, serene, sublime.

Riverside, St. Barnabas Day, 1849.

DE ¹GULIELMO MEO, MORTUO, SUSPIRIUM.

" Ah, my brother ! "

ALAS ! how life divides itself,
  The Left and the Departed ;
    Like funeral files, in double row,
  The Dead, the Broken-Hearted !

A DAISY,

FROM MY ENGLISH GOD-SON.

WHY should this little withered flower,
  So scentless, pale, and dry,
Be dearer than the garden's pride,
  That captivates the eye ?

It has a beauty for the mind,
  A fragrance for the heart,
Which time can no more dissipate,
  Than Nature could impart.

A precious little English boy,
  My own baptismal child,
An English daisy sent to me,
  Across the waters wild.

¹ William Croswell.

And English homes and English hearts,
  Through memory's magic power,
And all the blessed English Church,
  Live in that little flower.

Riverside, St. Matthew's Day, 1849.

————

THE OLD MAN OF VERONA,

WHO HAD NEVER BEEN BEYOND THE SUBURBS,

From the Latin of Claudian Epigram ii.

" Oh felice che mai non pose il piede
  Fuori della natia sua dolce terra ;
  Egli il cor non lascio fitto in oggetti
  Che di piu riveder on ha speranza,
  E cio, che vive ancor, morto, non piange."[1]

Pindemonte.

HAPPY the man, who spends his life, 'mid his paternal fields :
The roof which saw him cradled, to his age its shelter yields ;
And, where he crawled in infancy, he now, with staff in hand,
Scores the long tally of his years, upon the sunny sand.

[1] Happy the man who never roved
  Beyond his native land, beloved ;
  Whose heart is knit by no sad chain
  To those, he ne'er shall see again,
  Nor weeps the living, as the dead, and knows he weeps in vain.

G. W. D.

Not him with strange vicissitudes, has fortune drawn away,
Nor love of change e'er tempted him, by distant wave to ·
    stray.
No trader trembling on the sea, no soldier at the drum,
No lawyer, hoarse and weary, with the forum's ceaseless
    hum,
No *quidnunc*, he :[1] the nearest town, he never yet has seen ;
Too happy in his broad expanse of heaven, no wall between.
The years he reckons, not by kings, but by the crops they
    bring ;
He names each autumn, from its fruits, and from its flowers
    each spring.[2]
The plain, which hides his setting sun, brings back its rising
    light,
And all the world he knows, is that, which circles in his
    sight.
He well remembers each tall oak, since scarce it reached
    his knee,
And sees the whole coæval wood, grow old, as fast as he.
Neighb'ring Verona farther seems, than India's sunburnt
    strand,
And Lake Benacus is to him, the Red Sea, near at hand.
With vigour, all unbroken, and with shoulders broad and
    square,
His three times thirty years, still find him " none the worse
    for wear."

[1] " *Indocilis rerum;*" a man that does not read the papers. " *Quidnunc?*"—
" What news ?"

[2] As we say, " the last *peach year;*" "this will be an *apple year ;*" "a fine
dahlia season."

" Some love to roam ;" remotest Spain they seek, in strolling
    strife :
They " see the world," perhaps ; but *he* has much the most
    of life.

1850—1859.

LITTLE MARY'S GRAVE.

BORN, AUGUST 18, 1838, DIED, JAN. 13, 1844.

It was a sweet autumnal day ;
The rustling leaves, around me lay ;
The landscape, bathed in golden light,
As heaven itself, was fair and bright.

I waited for a funeral train :
And, sauntering through the Church-yard lane,
My thoughtful feet, instinctive, strayed,
To where a darling child was laid.
Sweet Mary ! I remember well,
How like a blessing, first, she fell ;
And on a joyous summer day,
Sweet flower, sweet bud, together lay.
And, well do I remember, too,
When wintry winds around us, blew,

We bore our summer bud, away,
Its sweetness, in the snow, to lay.
She was a most attractive child :
So gay, so free, so meek, so mild ;
A lovely, little, loving thing,
Among the heart-strings, made to cling.
Her childish fancy took to me :
She loved to hang upon my knee ;
And win, with many an artless wile,
The kiss that crowned the sunny smile.
I hear her flute-like accents, now,
I see the beaming, on her brow,
As from her little door-way seat,
She hailed, with glee, my passing feet,
As bright and glad, as any bird,
Could she but win one kindly word.

Sweet Mary, years have come, and gone,
Since last I heard thy loving tone ;
And time, and toil, and care, have shed
The snows of winter, on my head :
Yet, while I stand, beside thee, here,
And brush away the starting tear,
I hear, again, thy bird-like voice,
And, in thy childish love, rejoice.

Sweet Mary, thou art, now, with God !
We linger, yet, along the road :
Oh ! that the echoes of thy speech,
Our struggling hearts, from heaven, might reach ;

To win us, from the things of earth,
To thoughts and themes, of holier birth;
To teach us, to count all things loss;
For His dear sake, who bore the Cross:
That, all who loved thee, here, may be,
Through Him, at last, in Heaven, with thee!

1850.

THE FLIGHT INTO EGYPT.

"Out of Egypt have I called My Son."

MAIDEN mother, meek and mild,
Cherishing that cherub Child,
Why, through wild and weary way,
Should thy feeble footsteps stray?

Herod seeks the Loved One's life;
Glitters now the murderous knife;
Ramah, reeking lies, and red;
Rachel weeps her children, dead.

Maiden mother, meek and mild,
Fear not for thy cherub Child:
Through the wild and weary way,
Angel squadrons, with thee stay.

Hear what God, the Lord, hath done;
"Out of Egypt," called His Son;
Nailed Him to the atoning Tree;
Giv'n Him there, the victory.

Riverside, First Sunday after Epiphany, 1850.

———

THE MOTHER, AT THE GRAVE OF HER CHILD.

OUR little Mary is not dead; but, sweetly gone before,
She waits, to win, and welcome us, upon that happy shore;
To win us, with the memories, that linger, of her love;
And welcome us, to share, with her, the blessedness, above.

She is our little Mary, still, and never can grow old;
As young, as when the angel came, and took her, from our
    fold;
Made like unto the Mary-born, the only Undefiled,
She lives, in heaven's unchanging youth, our own immortal
    child.

Our dear ones, all, are growing up in beauty and in grace;
In manhood, and in womanhood, to fill, please God, their
    place;
But, whatsoever He may take, of all, that He has given,
One gift of His, we cannot lose, our little one in heaven.

Riverside, January 13, 1851.

FICUS RELIGIOSA.[1]

THE Banyan of the Indian Isles,
  Strikes deeply down, its massive root ;
And spreads its branching life, abroad,
  And bends, to earth, with scarlet fruit :
And, when the branches reach the ground,
  They firmly plant themselves, again :
Then rise, and spread, and drop, and root ;
  An ever green, and endless, chain.

And, so, the Church of Jesus Christ,
  The blessed Banyan of our God,
Fast rooted, upon Sion's Mount,
  Has sent its sheltering arms, abroad ;
And every branch, that, from it, springs,
  In sacred beauty, spreading wide,
As, low, it bends, to bless the earth,
  Still, plants another, by its side.

Long, as the world, itself, shall last,
  The sacred Banyan, still, shall spread ;
From clime to clime, from age to age,
  Its sheltering shadow shall be shed ;
Nations shall seek its " pillared shade,"
  Its leaves shall, for their healing, be :
The circling flood, that feeds its life,
  The blood, that crimsoned Calvary.

Riverside, 2d Sunday after Easter, 1851.

[1] Written for the third Jubilee of the Society for the Propagation of the Gospel.

WILLIAM CROSWELL,

POET, PASTOR, PRIEST.

ENTERED INTO LIFE, SUNDAY 9 NOVEMBER, 21 AFTER TRINITY, 1851.

I DID not think to number thee, my Croswell, with the
    'dead,
But counted on thy loving lips, to soothe my dying bed;
To watch the fluttering flood of life, ebb languidly away,
And point my spirit, to the gate, that opens into day.

My " more than brother " thou hast been, for five and
    twenty years,
In storm and shine, in grief and joy, alike in smiles and
    tears ;
Our twin-born hearts, so perfectly incorporate in one,
That not the shadow of a thought, e'er marred their unison.

Beside me, in life's highest noon, to hear the bridegroom's
    voice,
Thy loving nature fondly stood, contented to rejoice ;
Nor boon, that ever bounteous Heaven bestowed on me,
    or mine,
But bore for thee, a keener joy, than if it had been thine.

Thy fingers, at the sacred font, when God my hearth had
    blessed,
Upon my first-born's .brow, the dear baptismal sign, im-
    pressed ;

My second-born, thine own in Christ, our loving names to
    blend,
And knit, for life, his father's son, in with his father's
    friend.

And when our patriarchal White, with apostolic hands,
Committed to my trembling trust the Saviour's dread com-
    mands,
Thy manly form, and saintly face, were at my side
    again —
Thy voice, a trumpet to my heart, in its sincere *Amen !*

Beside thee once again, be mine, accepted priest, to
    stand,
And take, with thee, the pastoral palm, from that dear
    Shepherd's hand ;
As thou hast followed Him, be mine, in love, to follow
    thee,
Nor care, how soon my course be run ; so thine, my rest
    may be.

O beautiful and glorious death ! with all thy armour on ;
While, Stephen-like, thy placid face, out, like an angel's
    shone.
The words of blessing on thy lips, had scarcely ceased to
    sound,[1]
Before thy gentle soul, with them, its resting place had
    found.

[1] Unable to rise after the closing collect, he said the benediction on his knees.
He died in two hours.   A blood vessel was ruptured in his brain.

O pastoral and priestly death ! poetic as thy life—
A little child to shelter, in Christ's fold, from sin and
    strife ; [1]
Then, by the gate, that opens through the cross, for such
    as she,
To enter in thyself, with Christ, forevermore to be !

Riverside, November 10, 1851.

ROBIN REDBREAST.

I have, somewhere, met with an old legend, that a robin, hovering about the
Cross, bore off a thorn, from our dear Saviour's crown ; and dyed his bosom
with the blood ; and, that, from that time, robins have been the friends of
man.

SWEET Robin, I have heard them say,
That thou wert there, upon the day,
The Christ was crowned, in cruel scorn ;
And bore away, one bleeding thorn :
That, so, the blush, upon thy breast,
In shameful sorrow, was impressed ;
And, thence, thy genial sympathy,
With our redeemed humanity.

Sweet Robin, would that I might be,
Bathed, in my Saviour's blood, like thee ;

[1] He had just baptized an infant ; and his sermon was addressed to children.

Bear, in my breast, whate'er the loss,
The bleeding blazon of the Cross ;
Live, ever, with thy loving mind,
In fellowship, with human kind ;
And take my pattern, still, from thee,
In gentleness, and constancy.

Riverside, Conversion of St. Paul, 1852.

SARAH WALLACE GERMAIN,

**DIED AT ST. MARY'S HALL, ON THE EVE OF THE HOLY INNOCENTS, 1852
IN THE 15TH YEAR OF HER AGE.**

" These are they which follow the Lamb, whithersoever He goeth. "

WEEP not for her, the dear lamb we have folded,
    Safe from the serpent, secure from the bear ;
Gone to the source, where her being was moulded,
    She recks not of sorrow, and dreams not of care.
Through the green pastures, with skies ever vernal,
    By the still waters, her footsteps now rove ;
Led by the Shepherd, whose name is Eternal,
    Her loveliness lives in the light of His love.

Weep not for her, the dear lamb we have folded,
    Though sadly we miss her, from out our fond arms ;
Just when her young life had sweetly unfolded,
    And ours seemed renewed, in the life of her charms.

21

Here, for a while she has left us behind her,
  To wander and wait, on life's desolate shore ;
There, through the Cross, we shall certainly find her,
  And with her, the lambling we folded before.

THE CROSS;

FRAMED IN THE DOOR WHICH FRONTED MY SICK BED.

IN HOC SIGNO.

WRITTEN WITH MY CROSWELL'S PENCIL.

THAT blessed Cross — I bend mine eyes,
On its atoning sacrifice ;
And find forgiveness, from my God,
In its divine, redeeming, blood.

That blessed Cross — I tear my heart,
To make it, of myself a part ;
And gain no shelter, from my sin,
Till Christ be crucified, within.

That blessed Cross — I bow my life,
To bear its pain, its load, its strife ;
The way that leads me to my God,
The bleeding path my Saviour trod.

That blessed Cross, that blessed Cross,
Welcome, its wounds, its shame, its loss,
My hope, my help, my victory —
My Maker bore that Cross for me !

Newark, October 24, 1852.

THE BAPTISM OF TEARS.

TENTH SUNDAY AFTER TRINITY, AUGUST 15, 1802.

" They that sow in tears, shall reap in joy."

THE lovely day had passed away,
Its stillness, on the landscape lay ;
A summer sunset's lingering rays
Still kept the atmosphere, ablaze ;
When, gathered in a darkened room,
Where light just glimmered, through the gloom,
A sorrowing circle, silent sate ;
Distressed, but not disconsolate.

But yesterday, and every grace,
That makes of home, a sacred place,
The comforts, and the charms of life,
That blend in Mother, and in Wife ;

All that the heart of man holds dear,
Was crowned and consecrated here.
Serene and beautiful, to-day,
Decked for the dead, our darling lay ;
Whose eye, whose soul, whose heart, had been
The charm of all this sacred scene ;
So calm, so sweet, our blessed dead,
We scarce could deem the spirit fled.
Like infant, tired, that sinks to rest,
At noon upon its Mother's breast ;
Her score of summers scarcely done,
And yet her crown of victory won.
It is her own, her charmed room,
This ante-chamber of the tomb ;
Her Bible opens, at the day ;
The Book, that taught her how to pray,
Her Taylor, Kempis, Keble, lie
Just where she left them, all, to die.

In western window's deep retreat,
A table stands, in order meet,
With linen cloth, and roses white,
And crystal water, pure and bright.
The lingering beams of parting day,
Upon the trembling waters play ;
Then stretching through the glimmering gloom,
That fills the still, and sacred room,
Upon our dear one's forehead fall,
Like some celestial coronal ;
For sainted Mother, meet array,
To grace her babe's baptismal day.

Upon her fair and pulseless head,
His hand, the kneeling husband laid;
The honoured father bowed him low,
The mother's tears in silence flow,
From sisters, brothers, loved ones, friends,
The hushed and stifled sorrow blends;
One heart, one voice, in faltering flow,
Pours the low litany of woe,
" Thou gavest, Thou hast taken, Lord,
We bless Thy Holy name and Word!"

The surpliced Priest, comes gliding in;
The wave is blessed that saves from sin,
It sparkles on an infant's brow.
The child of grace and glory, now,
The Mother's blessed name is given,
That one may serve for both, in Heaven;
The cross is sealed, the pledge secured,
The heritage of Heaven, ensured;
The Mother's arms, the treasure, take,
With Jesu's mark, impressed, to nurse for Jesu's sake.

Scarce was the sacred service done,
And our dear dead one, left alone,
When whispering through the waving trees,
There came a balmy western breeze,
And strewed the rose-leaves, fair and white,
Upon the water, pure and bright,
As if some angel had been sent,
To certify the sacrament;

And flowers of love and peace been given,
To strew our darling's path to Heaven;
And way-marks left along the road,
To bring our baby, home to God.

Riverside, August 22, 1852.

"I HAVE FOUGHT WITH BEASTS AT EPHESUS."

"Have fought with beasts!" oh, blessed Paul,
How small were that, if that were all!
But harder far, to fight, with men,
Than beard the lions, in their den!

Men, who concert the secret snare,
To take the guileless, unaware;
Men, who, with "bated breath," betray,
And hint the things, they dare not say;

Men, who their sanctity proclaim,
In libels on a neighbour's name;
Men, who their nameless letters scrawl,
And chalk their scandal, on a wall;

Men, who will sit and eat your bread,
Then, lift their heel, to bruise your head;
Men, who abuse the holiest garb,
To hide the slanderer's poisoned barb.

But, Saviour, Thou hast known them all;
Peter, Iscariot, and Saul :
And, worse than all, Thy Father's face
Averted from Thee, for a space.

Why should the servant hope to be,
From ills, that haunt his Master, free ?
Who, the disciple, would accord,
A rule, less rigid, than his Lord ?

Then, Saviour, let me clasp Thy Cross,
And count all other things, but loss ;
Nor ask, from foes, to be set free ;
So, they be, also, foes to Thee !

Welcome the strife with godless men ;
The fight, with Satan in his den ;
One only thing, I crave, from Thee ;
Turn not Thy face, my God, from me !

"PERFECT, THROUGH SUFFERINGS."

HEB. II. 10.

"Perfect, through sufferings :" may it be,
Saviour, made perfect, thus, for me !
I bow, I kiss, I bless the rod,
That brings me nearer to my God.

" Perfect, through sufferings :" be Thy Cross
The crucible, to purge my dross !
Welcome, for that, its pangs, its scorns,
Its scourge, its nails, its crown of thorns.

" Perfect, through sufferings :" heap the fire,
And pile the sacrificial pyre ;
But spare each loved and loving one,
And let me feel the flames, alone.

" Perfect, through sufferings :" urge the blast,
More free, more full, more fierce, more fast ;
It recks not where the dust be trod,
So the flame waft my soul, to God.

The Breakers, June 1, 1853.

DELICIIS MEIS,

G. H. D.;

IN MARE NAVIGANTI.

WHEN morning streaks the eastern sky,
    And wakes the world for me ;
To thee, my first affections fly,
    My darling, on the sea.

Through all the close and crowded day,
    What toils, what cares, there be ;
By thee, my thoughts still find their way,
    My darling, on the sea.

While, from the far and fading West,
  The day dies duskily;
With thee, my spirit seeks its rest,
  My darling, on the sea.

The silent watches of the night,
  Still find my soul with thee;
And dreams restore thee, fond and bright,
  My darling, on the sea.

By day or night, in toil or rest,
  Whate'er my lot may be;
With thee, my fond heart finds its rest,
  My darling, on the sea.

And, come what can, of pains or cares,
  ' Of joys, or griefs, to me;
I still will shield thee, with my prayers,
  My darling, on the sea.

Riverside, August 30, 1852.

———

"RORES, FLORES."

WHEN April showers
Wake up the flowers,
  From their long winter's sleep,
The crocus starts,
The rose-bud parts,
  The fragrant violets peep.

22

When tear-drops fall,
At sorrow's call,
  On penitential heart,
The perfect peace,
That shall not cease,
  Like flowers in Spring, will start.

THE CHURCH OF THE HOLY INNOCENTS,

(IN ALBANY ;)

"A HOUSE OF PRAYER FOR ALL PEOPLE;"

Was Erected by a Childless Man, as the Memorial of his Four Dead Children.

In the Chancel, is a mural tablet, of the purest marble, with the simple record of their names and deaths, in four compartments, surrounded and separated by an exquisite wreath of lilies of the valley, the leaves and flowers, together ; the design of a young saint (the wife of the architect), who came from a Northern climate, to find, with us, an early grave.   At the foot of the tablet a lamb is sleeping, on the cross.

" Behold the lilies, how they grow."   "Of such, is the kingdom of God."

SWEET lilies of the valley, ye have been,
  From earliest childhood, my instinctive joy ;
And still, to meet you in the early Spring,
  My spirit leaps, as lithe, as when a boy !
The bells that seem to tinkle, with perfume,
  And spring, so jauntily, from those broad leaves ;
The purest white, upon the deepest green,
  That tricksome spring, in her embroidery weaves.

I've twined you, on the breast of blushing bride,
   And strewed you, on the hearse of coffined child ;
Till love grew fragrant, with a new delight,
   And childless sorrow kissed the rod, and smiled.
But, here, within this still and sacred aisle,
   Ye charm, anew, my meditative heart ;
Where mimic nature, in the marble blooms,
   And buried beauty lends a grace, to art.

Four lovely children glide, into the grave ;
   A childless father bends beneath the rod :
He makes their monument, a House of Prayer ;
   The gold, he meant for them, he gives to God.
Upon a tablet of the purest white,
   Enwreathed with lilies, he records his loss ;
Their innocence, he emblems, with his faith ;
   A lamb, recumbent, sleeps upon the cross.

Lake Ontario, August 6, 1853.

THE CHRISTIAN PILGRIM—BY CRAWFORD.

TO S. P. C.

SWEET maiden, I would be like thee,
   As heavenward, eye, and thought, and heart ;
And foot, as lightly, to the earth,
   Like greyhound, straining on the start ;

As closely to the Cross, I'd cling,
  And lean as simply on its stay ;
The things of earth, all thistle down,
  As hindrances, along my way.

Sweet maiden, by that scollop shell,
  Thy thoughts are where the Saviour lay ;
And towards His tomb, thy steps are bent,
  To wait, and watch, and weep, and pray ;
And I, my heart, would bury, there,
  As dead to self, as dead to sin ;
With thee, His Cross, on earth, to bear,
  With thee, His Crown, in heaven, to win.

1853.

TO ONE OF RAPHAEL'S ANGELS.[1]

" Take heed that ye despise not one of these little ones; for I say unto you,
that in heaven their angels do always behold the face of my FATHER which
is in heaven."

SWEET angel, while I gaze on thee,
  So mute, so meek, so mild,
I deem that thou must surely be
  The angel of some child ;
To whom the SAVIOUR said, such grace,
  For our sakes, has been given,
That they behold the FATHER's face,
  Continually in Heaven.

[1] That one of the two at the foot of the *Madonna di S. Sisto*, which is
leaning on both arms.

Sweet angel, I would be like thee,
   In faith, in hope, in love ;
My heart's affections, constantly,
   Engaged with things above ;
My thoughts, turned off from earth, like thine,
   " Commercing with the skies,"
Till all the Majesty Divine
   Grow radiant, to mine eyes.

Sweet angel, I will ever pray,
   To JESUS meek and mild,
That I may be, from day to day,
   Still more, His " little child."
So, through the Cross, such grace to me,
   May graciously be given,
That thou for me, may'st always see
   My FATHER's face, in Heaven.

The Breakers, June, 1853.

TO MY SWEET GRAND-DAUGHTER,

ELIZA GREENE DOANE,

ON HER BAPTISMAL BIRTH-DAY.

SWEET baby, when thy father
   Was granted to our love,
We hailed him, as a blessed streak
   Of sunshine, from above :

And all his life, he still has shed
    His sunshine, on our way :
And cheered us, with his brightness,
    Through the dark, and cloudy day.

Now, two and twenty winters
    Have heaped on us their snows :
And, down the hill of life, our feet
    Are tottering to repose :
When, once again, the love of God,
    Upon our path, has smiled,
In the sunshine of our sunshine,
    Our Willie's darling child.

Thou meek and gentle Jesus,
    We bring her to be Thine :
Baptized into the blessed Name,
    Of the eternal Trine :
And humbly, we implore Thy grace,
    To keep her for Thine own ;
And guide us all, to meet, at last,
    Before Thy glorious throne.

Riverside, St. Andrew's Day, 1854.

A PRAYER.

FATHER, to Thy hands I give,
Her in whom my soul doth live ;

To her feet be Thou the guide,
Be the buckler by her side :
All the day from harm to keep,
All the night to guard her sleep ;
Warding evil from her heart,
 Bidding shapes of ill depart;
Making truth and innocence
Still her solace and defence ;
Till, by grace, thro' faith, she be
Taken home to dwell with Thee.

FANNY'S GRAVE.

There's pansies, that's for thoughts."—Ophelia, in Hamlet.
" A most unspotted lily." —Cranmer, in Henry VIII.

UPON our darling Fanny's grave,
  The Pansies are in bloom :
What sweetest thoughts, unbidden, spring,
  Beside her sacred tomb !
Forever, shall my memory dwell,
  Upon that peaceful spot :
For one, so loved, my faithful heart
  Needs no " forget me not ! "

The lilies of the valley wave,
  At Fanny's dearest feet :
While she, on flowers immortal, treads,
  A thousand times more sweet.

Still may her loveliness attract
  Our thoughts, and hearts above ;
Till, through the Cross she clasped, we join
  The Lily of our love !

Whitsunday, 1855.

————

THE NEW CRADLE.

*A very little boy, whose infant brother had died the day before, being asked
where he was, sweetly replied, "Asleep, up stairs, in his new cradle."*

" ASLEEP, in his new cradle "—
  How beautiful the thought,
Thy childhood, in its simpleness,
  From nature's heart, has caught :
A reach, our " Sweetest Shakespeare,"
  Himself, has failed to win ;
And one, whose truthful tenderness
  Must make " the world, all kin."

" Asleep, in his new cradle "—
  Sad mother, dry your tears ;
In this, your heart-bereavement,
  God's tenderest love appears :
The cradle, you provided,
  From death, could not be free ;
Your loveliest has now secured
  His immortality.

" Asleep, in his new cradle "—
   He wakes in Paradise ;
The lullabies of nature,
   Lost, in its symphonies :
Among the holy children,
   In pastures green, he plays ;
Or joins, with lisping accents,
   In the music of their lays.

" Asleep in his new cradle "—
   He waits for you to come,
From earth, its sins and sorrows,
   To his bright and happy home ;
Till the resurrection-breaking,
   God's loved ones, all, shall bring,
And the dead in Christ, awaking,
   Reign with their Saviour-King.

Riverside, Septuagesima, 1855.

THE EYES OF THE ANGELS.

A little child was disappointed, when her mother told her what the stars were.
She said, " I thought they were the eyes of angels."

" MOTHER, what are those little things,
   That twinkle from the skies ? "
" The Stars, my child ! " " I thought, Mother,
   They were the angels' eyes.
     23

" They look down on me, so like yours,
     As beautiful, and mild ;
When, by my crib, you used to sit,
     And watch your feverish child.

" And, always, when I shut my eyes,
     And said my little prayers,
I felt so safe : because I knew,
     That they had opened theirs. "

Riverside, Monday before Easter, 1855.

----

¹" MY LOVE LIES BLEEDING. "

THAT melancholy Amaranth ;
     It haunts me all the day,
With memories of " my birdie love, "
     Now " flying, " far away.
" Where is ' my precious baby' gone ? "
     Rings out, on all the air ;
And stillness stuns my ear, the while ;
     Till echo answers " where ? "

My Lizzie " birdie " nestles, now,
     Upon the sounding shore ;
Yet, still, her flute-notes sweet, I hear,
     Through all the breakers' roar :

¹ The common name, for the flower, known to botanists, as " Amaranthus Melancholicus ; " a favorite flower of the little grand-child, to whom these lines were written.   The words in quotation, in these two *songs,* are the baby language that they used together.

And, when she spreads her dovelike wings,
  The foaming surge, to brave :
With plumes, like "yellow gold, " she seems
  An angel on the wave.

That melancholy Amaranth,
  With pendant, purple flowers,
    Like weeping-willow, stands to mark,
  The graves of parted hours.
Far, far away, " my birdie love "
  Is " plashing " in the sea ;
" My love lies bleeding, " all that's left,
  To solitude and me.

August 15, 1856.

FROM "DANPY" TO HIS "BIRDIE."

WITH A WINTER BLOSSOM.[1]

My " birdie " love, your little flowers
  Have touched your " Danpy's " heart ;
And made the tears, like April drops,
  From its deep fountains, start.

He laid the fair and fragrant things,
  Between his Prayer Book leaves :
To look at in his loneliness ;
  And cheer him, when he grieves.

[1] A curl of his hair.

So may his "birdie Lizzie" lie
    Safe, in the Church's arms ;
Still guarded, by her watchful love,
    And kept from sins and harms :

Till, at the gracious Saviour's call,
    She spreads her golden wings :
And, in the paradise of God,
    Forever flies and sings !

Ascension, 1856.

THE HEART NEED NOT GROW OLD.

THERE are who deem life's afternoon,
    At best a dark and dreary time,
Too late to yield a second bloom,
    Too chill to keep the flowers of prime ;
That day by day, and step by step,
    While friends of youth, beside us fall,
The weary heart, grown dull with age
    Responds no more to friendship's call.

Believe them not, my gentle girl,
    Those libellers of love and truth,
Nor let the clouds of coming years,
    O'ercast the spring-time of thy youth.
The light of sense may all go out,
    And passion's wild-fire quite grow cold.
But time chills not the warmth of truth,
    The loving heart grows never old.

TO THE SWEET ¹DAUGHTERS OF THE CROSS;

WHO WROUGHT, FOR ME, THE EVERGREEN, ²EMBLEM OF OUR SALVA-
TION.

" Only in the Cross."

SWEET children, in the Cross, you bring,
  Three lessons, I discern :
For, though I'm nearly sixty years,
  I'm not too old to learn.

It teaches me, that, for my sins,
  My God was crucified :
Incarnate as the Virgin's Son,
  The Lord of glory died.

It teaches me, that I must bear
  His painful, shameful Cross ;
And count, for Him, myself, the world,
  And all things else, but loss.

It teaches me, that fadeless wreaths,
  For faithful ones, are twined ;
When, through the Spirit's guiding love,
  Their homes, in heaven, they find.

¹ The pupils of St. Mary's Hall.

² This same cross, that, for so many years, had told him of his children's
Christmas love, was laid on this, " first Christmas without their Father," among
the flowers that bloomed that day upon his grave.

. Sweet children, learn these lessons, now ;
    The bleeding Cross, hold fast ;
Endure its load, in patient love ;
    And wear the Crown, at last.

PRAY FOR YOUR PASTOR.

" DEAREST BISHOP,— Dr. N. preached his first sermon, as our Rector, yesterday ; and may I not ask your prayers that his ministry may be blessed to our
eternal good."

PRAY for your Pastor ! — that I will ;
That, his great trust, he may fulfil,
    To feed the flock of God :
The lost, to seek ; the young to train ;
The timid, cheer ; the bold, restrain ;
    With pastoral staff and rod.

Pray for your Pastor ! — that, I do :
That all his words be wise and true ;
    And all his prayers sincere ;
His teachings, what the Church approves ;
His conduct, such as Jesus loves ;
    His conscience, always clear.

Pray for your Pastor ! — certainly ;
Else, what a Bishop I should be !
    How else, the trial meet ;
When, at the throne of Christ, I stand,
Pastors and flocks, on either hand,
    To lay them at His feet.

Sweet soul, your Bishop needs your prayers,
In all his trials, toils and cares,
   His watchings and his tears :
And, ask your Pastor's, for him, too ;
That he may stand, erect and true,
   When Christ, the Judge appears.

Riverside, September 19, 1857.

LINES SENT, WITH A BIBLE,

To my wife.

Go, Holy Book, to her, my soul,
   Of earthly treasures, holds most dear,
Go, cheer with joy the sorrowing heart,
   With hope, the clouded vision clear.

Be to her fainting spirit, strength,
   Be light before her faltering feet,
Give humble faith, give heavenly might,
   To seek, to reach the mercy-seat.

And Thou, divine and gentle Dove,
   Let not Thy gracious strivings cease ;
Fire Thou her soul, with sacred love,
   Fill Thou her soul, with perfect peace.

Our Father hear thy children's prayer —
Our griefs removed, our sins forgiven,
Build Thou again, and bless, our home,
And fit us there, for Thee, and Heaven.

TO MISS STANLEY'S SUNDAY–MORNING BIRD :

For several mornings, a little bird found its way into the saloon at St. Mary's Hall, where a Sunday class was gathered.

LITTLE wingéd bit of song.
Wheresoe'er thou dost belong,
Come, and go, without a fear ;
Thou art ever welcome here !

Dost thou know the sacred day ?
Dost thou know where maidens pray ?
Wast thou won down, from the sky,
By our Chapel minstrelsy ?

Did the angels tell thee, when
Thou might'st hear good Bishop Ken,[1]
In that sweetest Morning Hymn
Fit for chanting Cherubim !

[1] Bishop Ken's " Morning Hymn" is always sung on Sundays, in the Chapel of the Holy Innocents ; also the Evening Hymn.

Did the Saviour, from above,
In the fulness of His love,
Send a message down, by thee ;
" Let the children come to Me ?"

Little wingéd bit of song,
Wheresoe'er thou dost belong,
Come, and go, without a fear !
•   Thou art ever welcome here !

August, 1858.

THE WEDDED FLAGS:

A SONG OF THE ATLANTIC CABLE.

HANG out that glorious old red cross !
    Hang out the stripes and stars !
They faced each other fearlessly,
    In two historic wars.

But now, the ocean circlet binds
    The bridegroom, and the bride :
Old England, young America —
    Display them, side by side.

24

High up, from Trinity's tall spire,
    We'll fling the banners out ;
Hear how the world-wide welkin rings,
    With that exulting shout.

Forever wave, those wedded flags,
    As proudly now they wave !
God, for the lands, His love has blessed,
    The beauteous, and the brave.   •

But see ! the dallying wind, the stars,
    About the cross, has blown ;
And see, again, the cross, around
    The stars its folds has thrown.

Was ever sign so beautiful,
    Hung from the heavens, abroad ?
Old England, young America,
    For freedom, and for God.

TO MARGARET HARRISON DOANE,

BAPTIZED ST. MICHAEL AND ALL ANGELS, MDCCCLVIII.

"Are they not all ministering spirits, sent forth to minister for them which
shall be heirs of salvation ?"

MARGARET, sweetest — that means, *Pearl*—
You are, now, a Christian girl ;

[1] The English and American flags, displayed together from the spire of
Trinity Church, New York, on the day of "the Cable Celebration," were
blown across each other in mutual embrace.

In the pure, baptismal wave,
Sin and death have found a grave ;
Through the blood of Him, who died :
Christ, for sinners, crucified.

Sweetest Margaret, darling girl,
Be, henceforth, the Saviour's pearl !
This is all the Angels' day ;
Excellent, in strength are they ;
Made, in Christ, salvation's heir,
You are, now, the Angels' care.

Margaret, darling, sweetest girl,
Seek, in Christ, the priceless pearl.
Be a pearl, in holiness ;
Be a pearl, in preciousness ;
Then, forevermore be set,
In the Saviour's coronet.

Riverside, September 29, 1858.

THE FIRST GREEN.

ON MY MOTHER'S GRAVE, IN SWEET ST. MARY'S CHURCHYARD.

"I went heavily : as one that mourneth for his mother."

IT was wintry, dearest Mother, when we left you to your
rest,
In the sweet and sacred shadow, which you always loved
the best ;

The snow lay all about us, in its dreariness and chill,
And your children turned away from you, with hearts more
    dreary, still.

Through the flocks my Master trusts me with, I've wan-
    dered far and nigh,
And return, to find, that Spring has set its blueness in the
    sky ;
And shed its twinkling laughter, on the glad and glancing
    wave ;
And, dearer to my heart, than all, its greenness, on your
    grave.

How well do I remember, the grass-plat that you made ;
And studded it, with violets, beneath a plum-tree's shade ;
And led me there, each sweet Spring morn, and watched
    me at my play ;
And taught me, at the sunset, by your knees, to kneel, and
    pray.

Almost threescore years, my Mother, have glided by, since
    then ;
And, a child, in all but innocence, I kneel, by you, again ;
With violets, and with pansies, I perfume the sacred sod ;
While I pray for grace, to join you, in the paradise of God.

   St. Mary's Churchyard, April 17, 1858.

THE ALL SAINTS FLOWERS,

With the Autumn leaves, from the Altar of the Chapel of St. Barnabas, were
laid, by the Priest, after the service on his grand-mother's grave.

SWEET flowers upon my mother's grave,
   Ye glad my eye and heart ;
For ye were always her delight,
   And of her life, a part.
No roses ever bloomed like hers ;
   No lilies were so sweet ;
And pansy, jasmine, mignonette,
   Ran riot, at her feet.

She treads a fairer garden now ;
   The Paradise of God :
And, walks, with reverent step, and slow,
   Where Jesu's feet have trod ;
Reclines, beside the crystal streams,
   On banks of asphodel ;
And, with the throng of saints, delights,
   The Saviour's love to tell.

Sweet flowers, to which, the Altar, first,
   Its consecration, lent ;
By filial hands, in grateful love,
   So beautifully blent ;
Ye mind me of my mother's care,
   Which overflowed on me ;
And, on my children, shed the grace,
   Of its benignity.

Sweet mother, these Autumnal leaves,
  With hectic beauty, bright,
Tell how, through long and lingering years,
  You faded on our sight;
And, then, they tell, of that bright time,
  When God, His saints shall bring;
And heaven's own beauty all, be thine —
  The Resurrection Spring.

All Saints Day, 1858.

THE FIRST CHRISTMAS,

WITHOUT MY MOTHER.

"One who mourneth for his mother."

SWEET Mother, eight and fifty years,
  Thy Christmas blessings crowned my brow;
Thy seat is vacant, by my side;
  And Christmas comes, without thee, now.

A shadow creeps, across my hearth;
  The cypress twines the holly-bough;
I cannot frame the Christmas phrase:
  For Christmas comes, without thee, now.

Along the line of threescore years,
　　In gifts and prayers, like tracks in snow,
I trace thy ever-living love :
　　But Christmas comes, without thee, now.

And yet, sweet Mother, though the thought
　　Will choke and tear, my bursting breast ;
And tears o'ercast this joyous day ;
　　I would not call thee, from thy rest.

Safe in the Paradise of God,
　　Thy home is with the holy dead ;
Where Christmas boughs are ever green ;
　　And the Christ-feast is always spread.

Christmas, 1858.

INDEX.

25